FAR OUT
FOLKTALES

STONE ARCH BOOKS
a capstone imprint

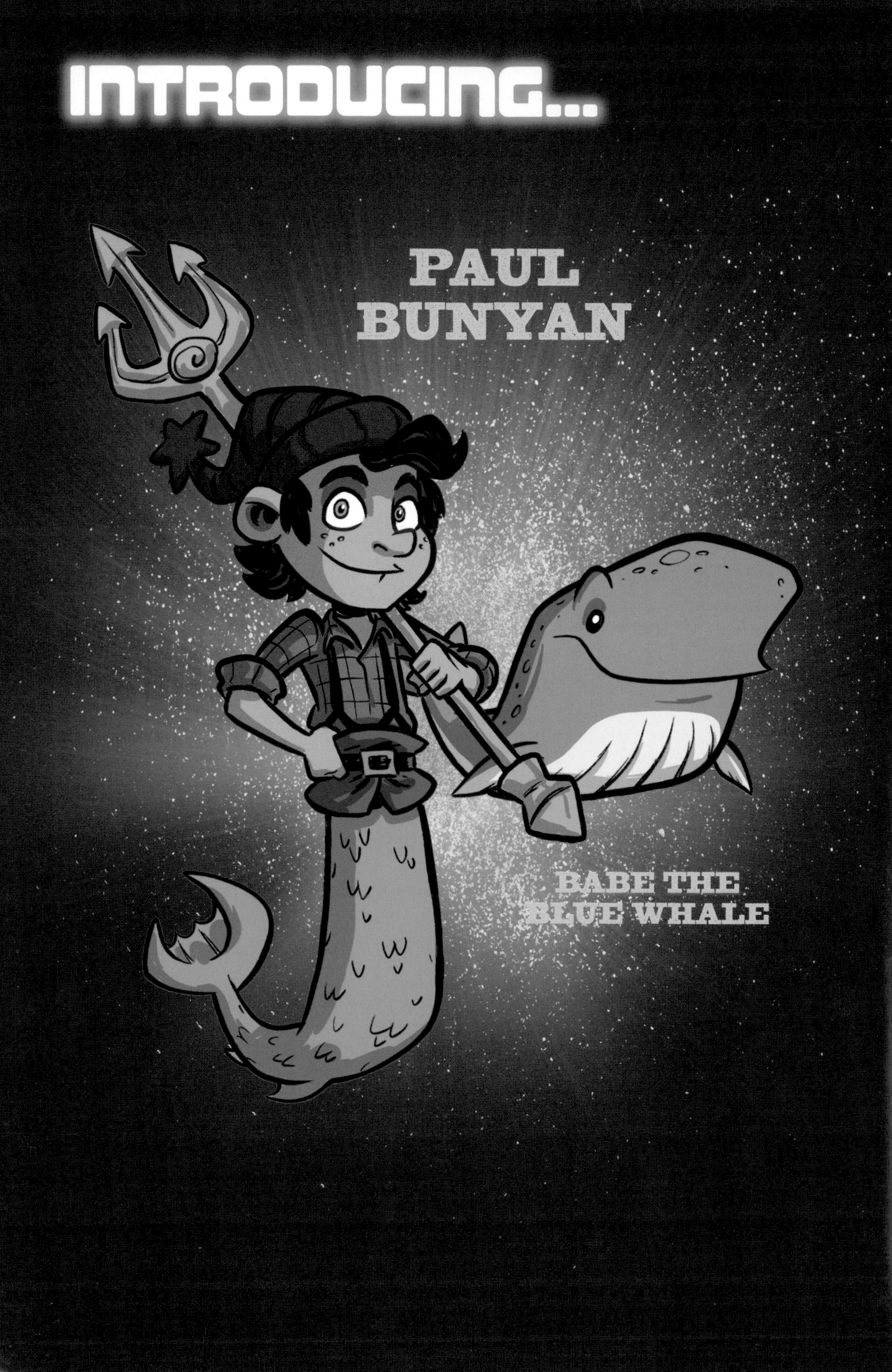
INTRODUCING...
PAUL
BUNYAN
BABE THE
BLUE WHALE

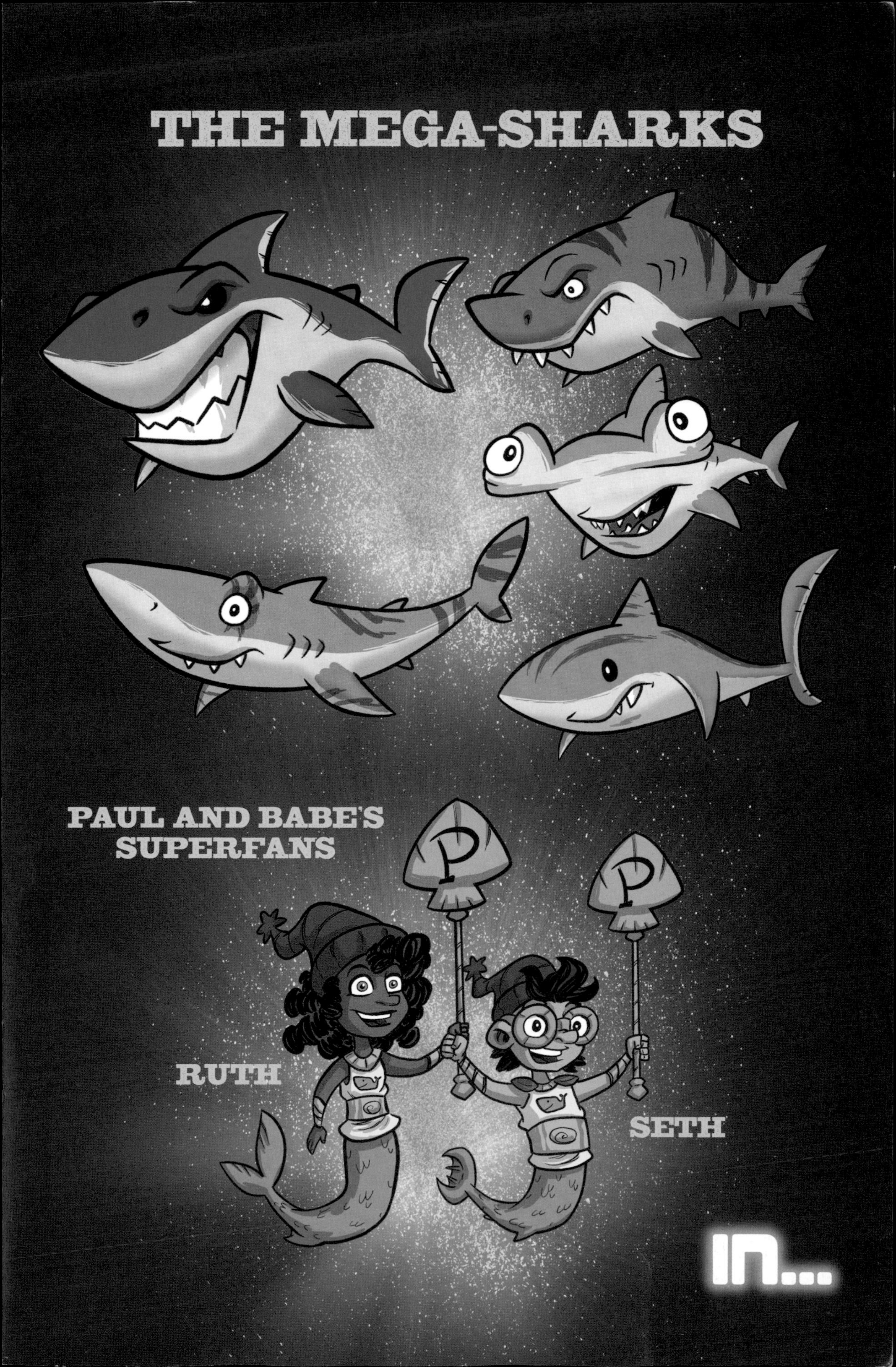
THE MEGA-SHARKS
PAUL AND BABE'S SUPERFANS
RUTH
SETH
IN...

Far Out Folktales is published by
Stone Arch Books
A Capstone Imprint
1710 Roe Crest Drive
North Mankato, Minnesota 56003
www.mycapstone.com

Cataloging-in-Publication Data is
available at the Library of Congress
website.
ISBN 978-1-4965-7842-6 (hardcover)
ISBN 978-1-4965-8007-8 (paperback)
ISBN 978-1-4965-7847-1 (eBook PDF)

Summary: In Atlantis, there aren't any
merfolk taller or mightier than Paul
Bunyan. The merboy has already dragged
the city away from an underwater
volcano and rescued a baby blue whale.
But now the hero is face-to-face with
a danger as big as him . . . . a mob of
mega-sharks! Can Paul use his huge size
and massive smarts to save the day?

Designed by Brann Garvey
Edited by Abby Huff
Lettered by Jaymes Reed

Printed and bound in China.
966

FAR OUT FOLKTALES

PAUL BUNYAN AND BABE THE BLUE WHALE

A GRAPHIC NOVEL

by **Penelope Gruber**
illustrated by **Otis Frampton**

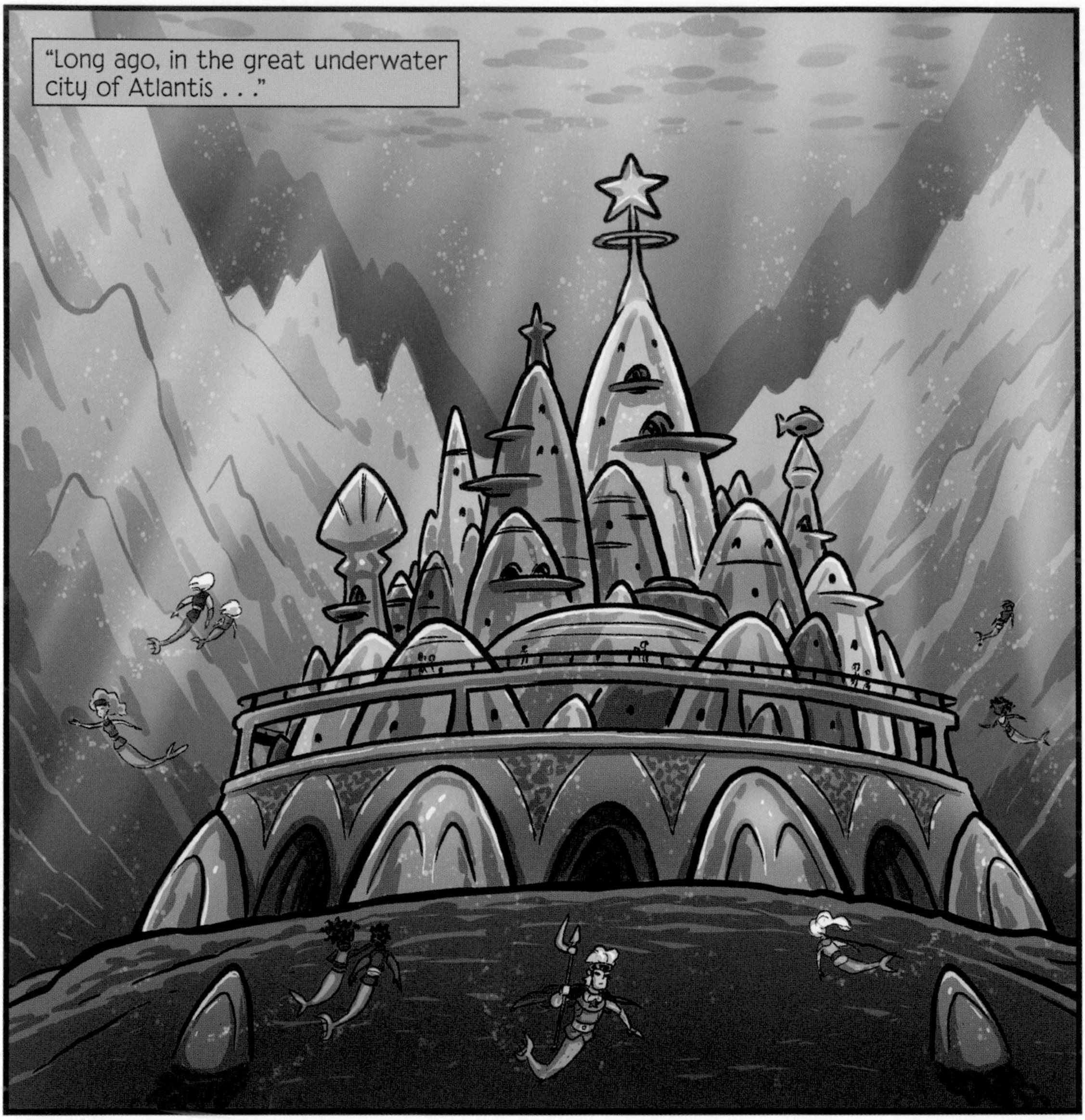
"Long ago, in the great underwater city of Atlantis . . ."

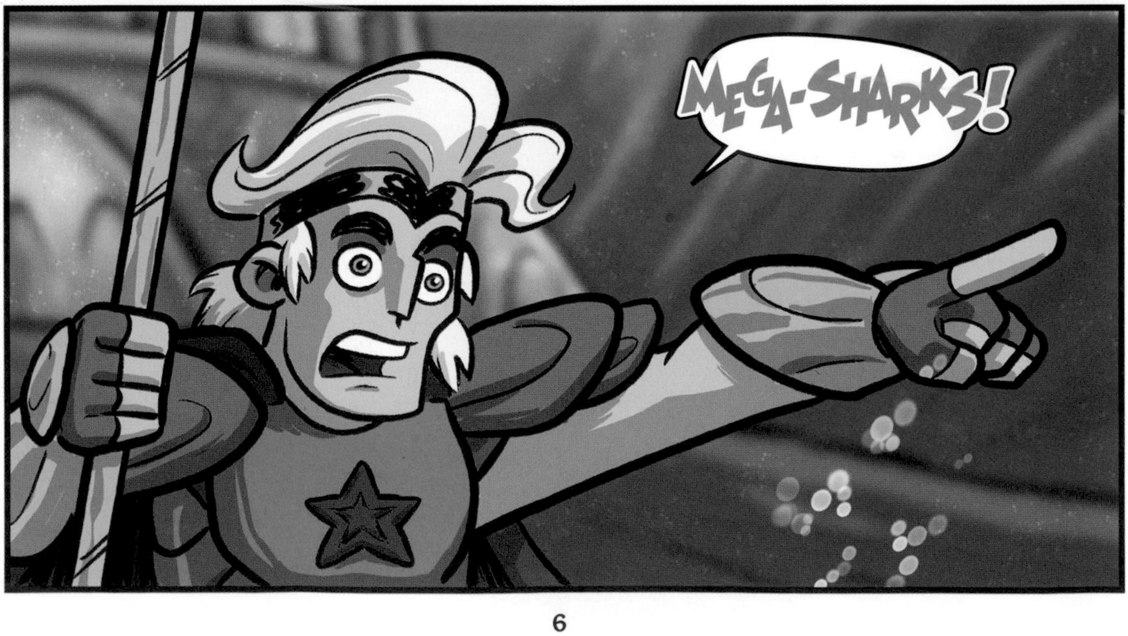
MEGA-SHARKS!

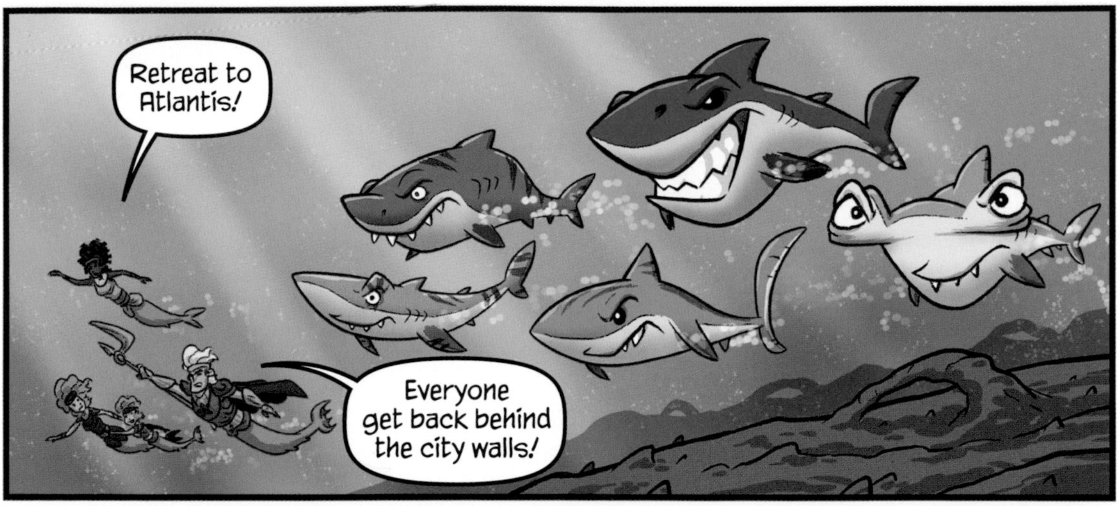
Retreat to Atlantis!
Everyone get back behind the city walls!

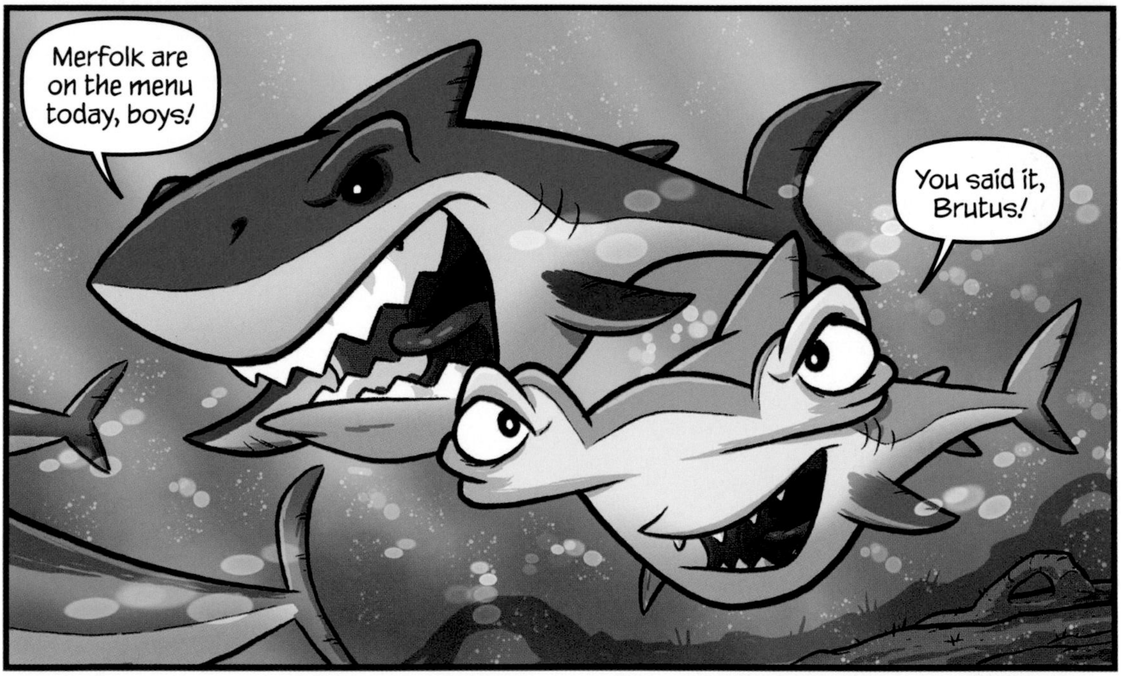
Merfolk are on the menu today, boys!
You said it, Brutus!

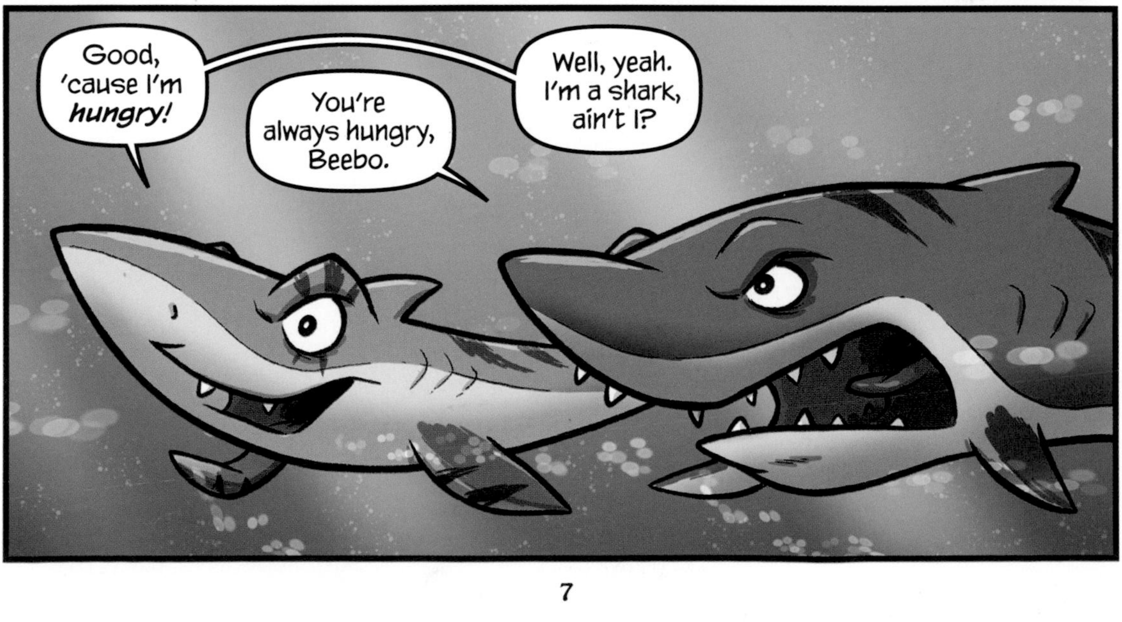
Good, 'cause I'm *hungry*!
You're always hungry, Beebo.
Well, yeah. I'm a shark, ain't I?

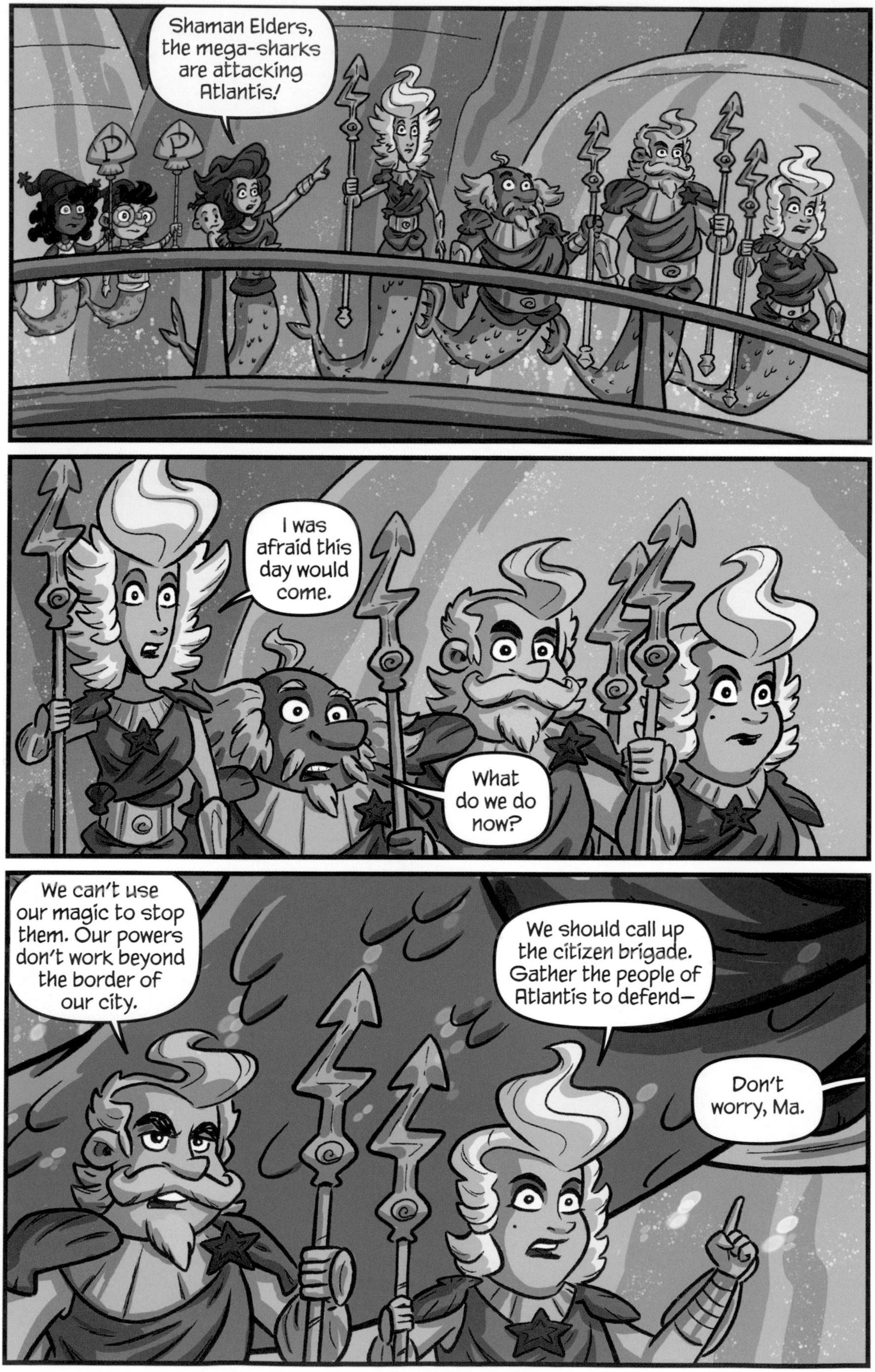
Shaman Elders, the mega-sharks are attacking Atlantis!
I was afraid this day would come.
What do we do now?
We can't use our magic to stop them. Our powers don't work beyond the border of our city.
We should call up the citizen brigade. Gather the people of Atlantis to defend—
Don't worry, Ma.

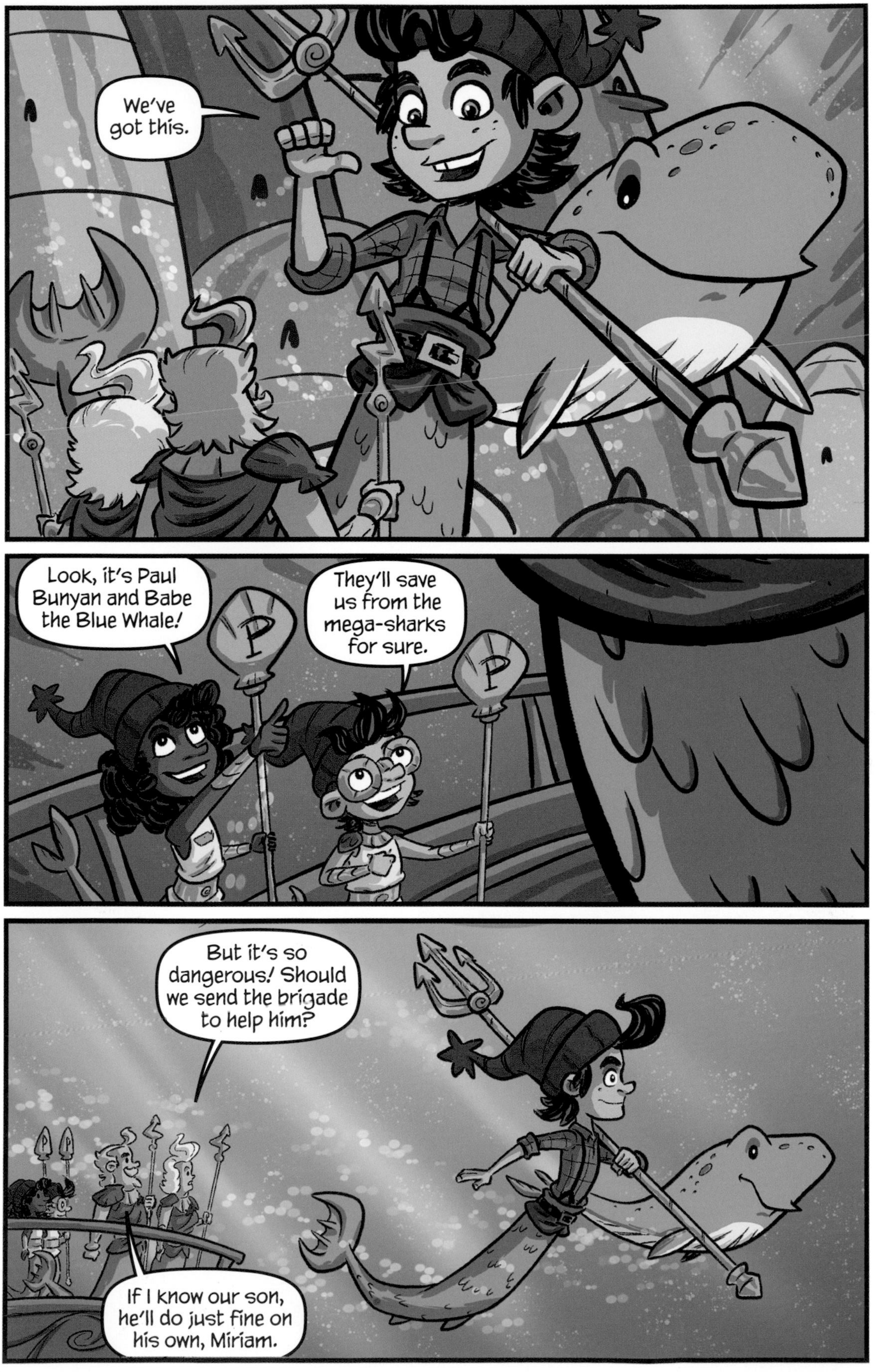
We've got this.
Look, it's Paul Bunyan and Babe the Blue Whale!
They'll save us from the mega-sharks for sure.
But it's so dangerous! Should we send the brigade to help him?
If I know our son, he'll do just fine on his own, Miriam.

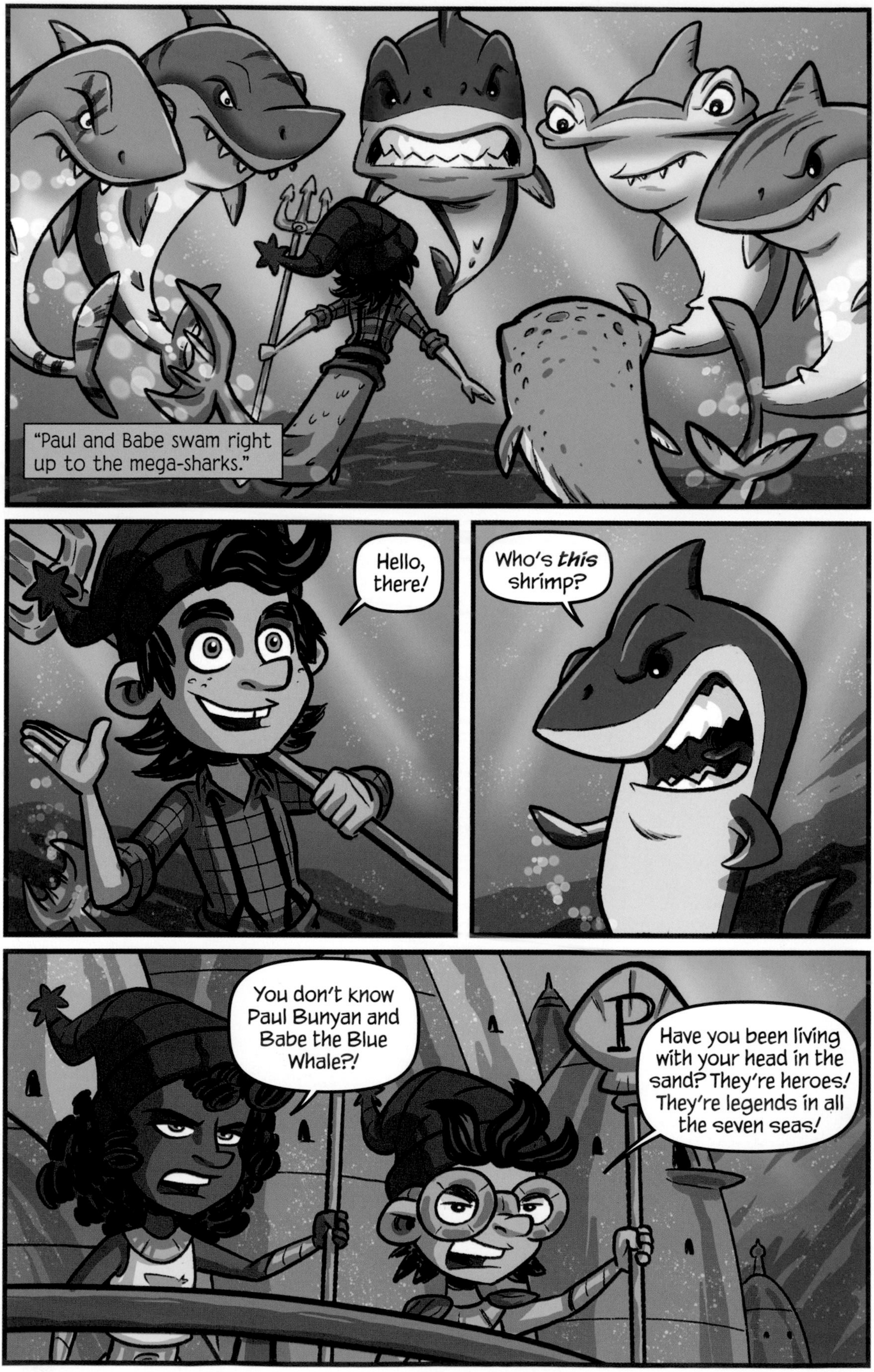
"Paul and Babe swam right up to the mega-sharks."
Hello, there!
Who's *this* shrimp?
You don't know Paul Bunyan and Babe the Blue Whale?!
Have you been living with your head in the sand? They're heroes! They're legends in all the seven seas!
P

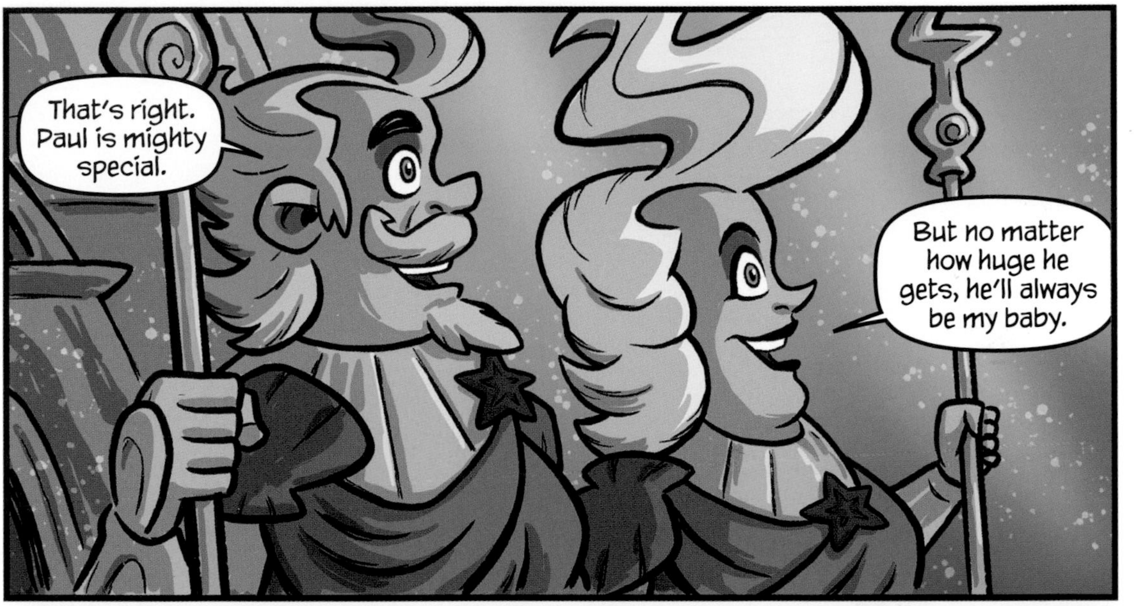
That's right. Paul is mighty special.
But no matter how huge he gets, he'll always be my baby.

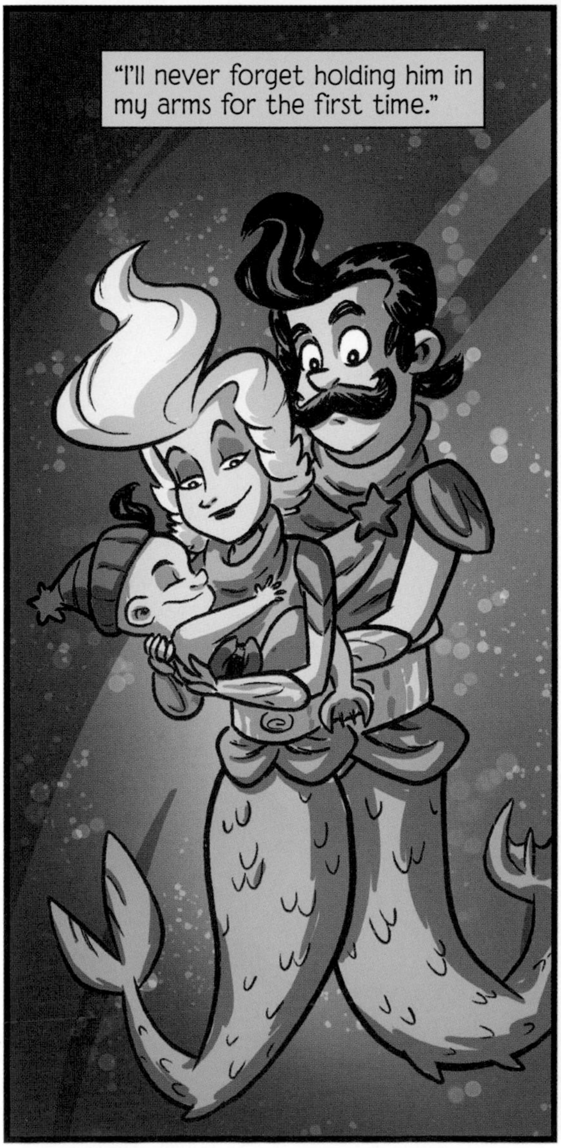
"I'll never forget holding him in my arms for the first time."

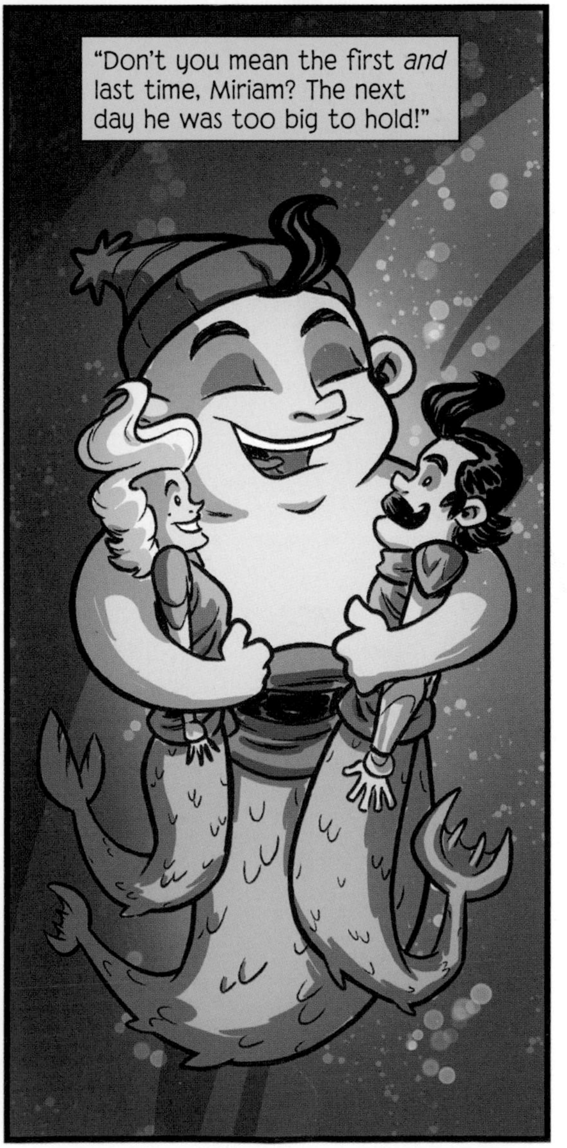
"Don't you mean the first *and* last time, Miriam? The next day he was too big to hold!"

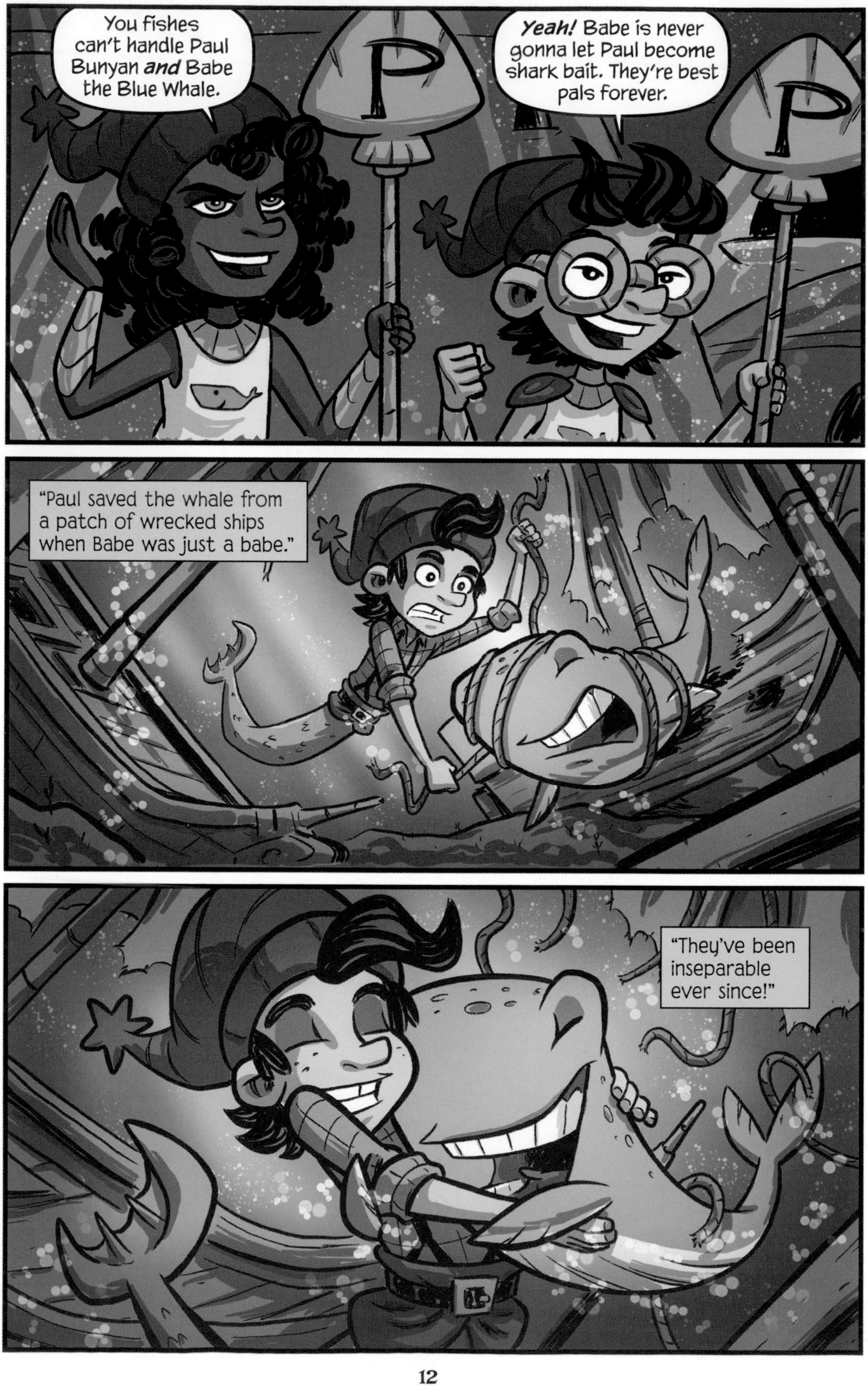

You fishes can't handle Paul Bunyan *and* Babe the Blue Whale.
Yeah! Babe is never gonna let Paul become shark bait. They're best pals forever.
"Paul saved the whale from a patch of wrecked ships when Babe was just a babe."
"They've been inseparable ever since!"

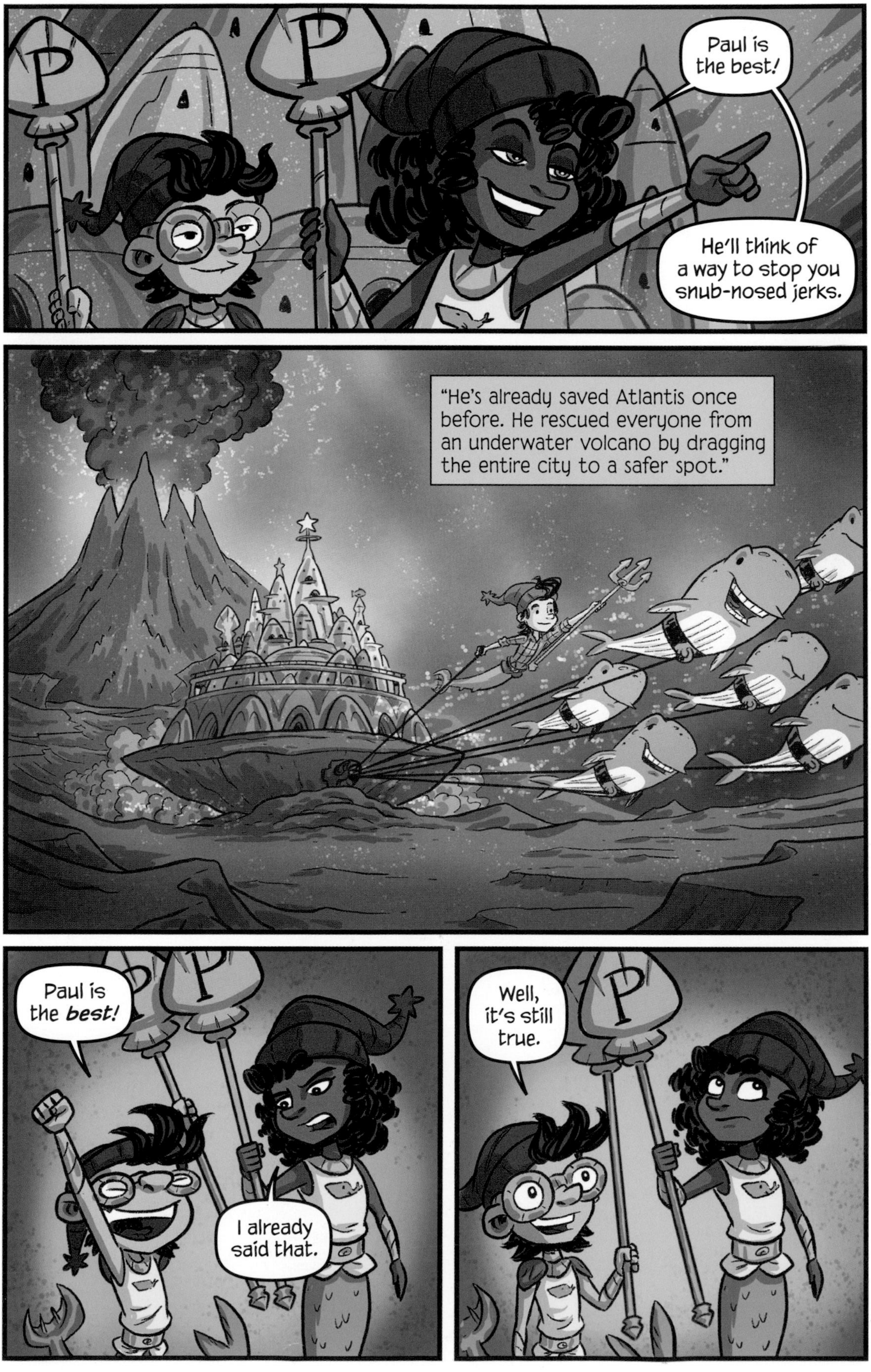
Paul is the best!
He'll think of a way to stop you snub-nosed jerks.
"He's already saved Atlantis once before. He rescued everyone from an underwater volcano by dragging the entire city to a safer spot."
Paul is the best!
I already said that.
Well, it's still true.

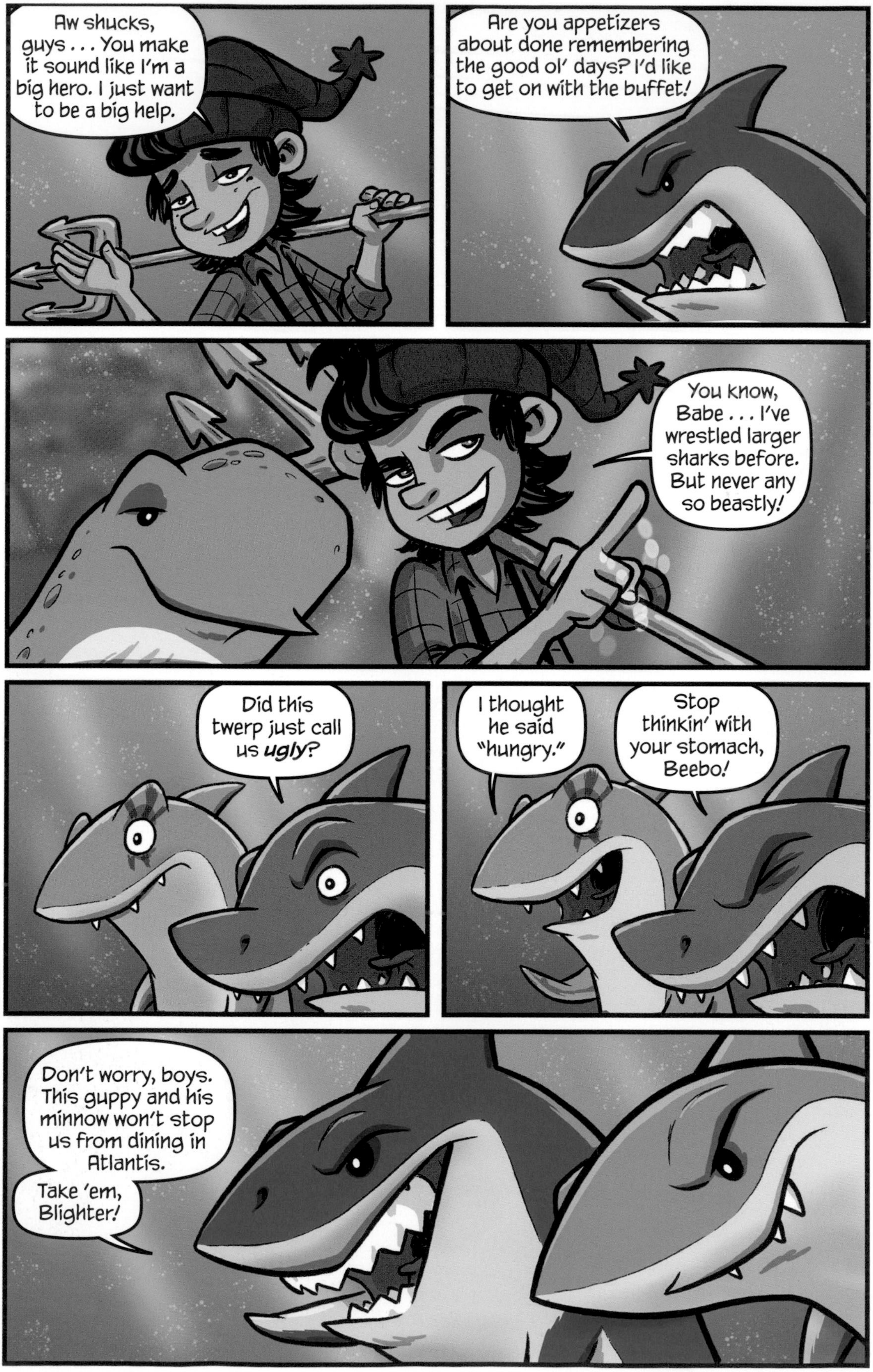
Aw shucks, guys . . . You make it sound like I'm a big hero. I just want to be a big help.
Are you appetizers about done remembering the good ol' days? I'd like to get on with the buffet!
You know, Babe . . . I've wrestled larger sharks before. But never any so beastly!
Did this twerp just call us *ugly*?
I thought he said "hungry."
Stop thinkin' with your stomach, Beebo!
Don't worry, boys. This guppy and his minnow won't stop us from dining in Atlantis.
Take 'em, Blighter!

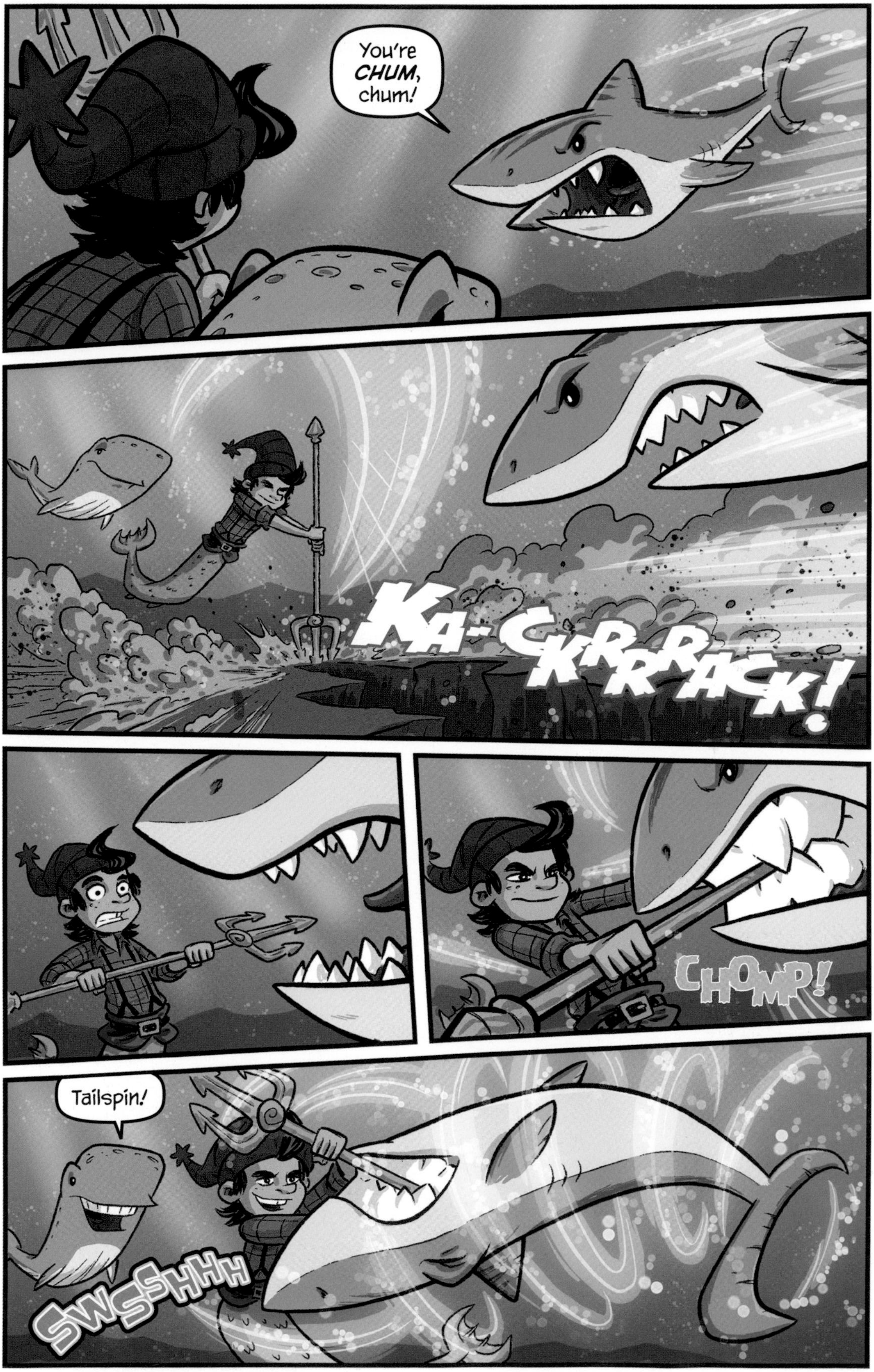

You're CHUM, chum!
KA-CKRRRRACK!
CHOMP!
Tailspin!
SWSSHHH

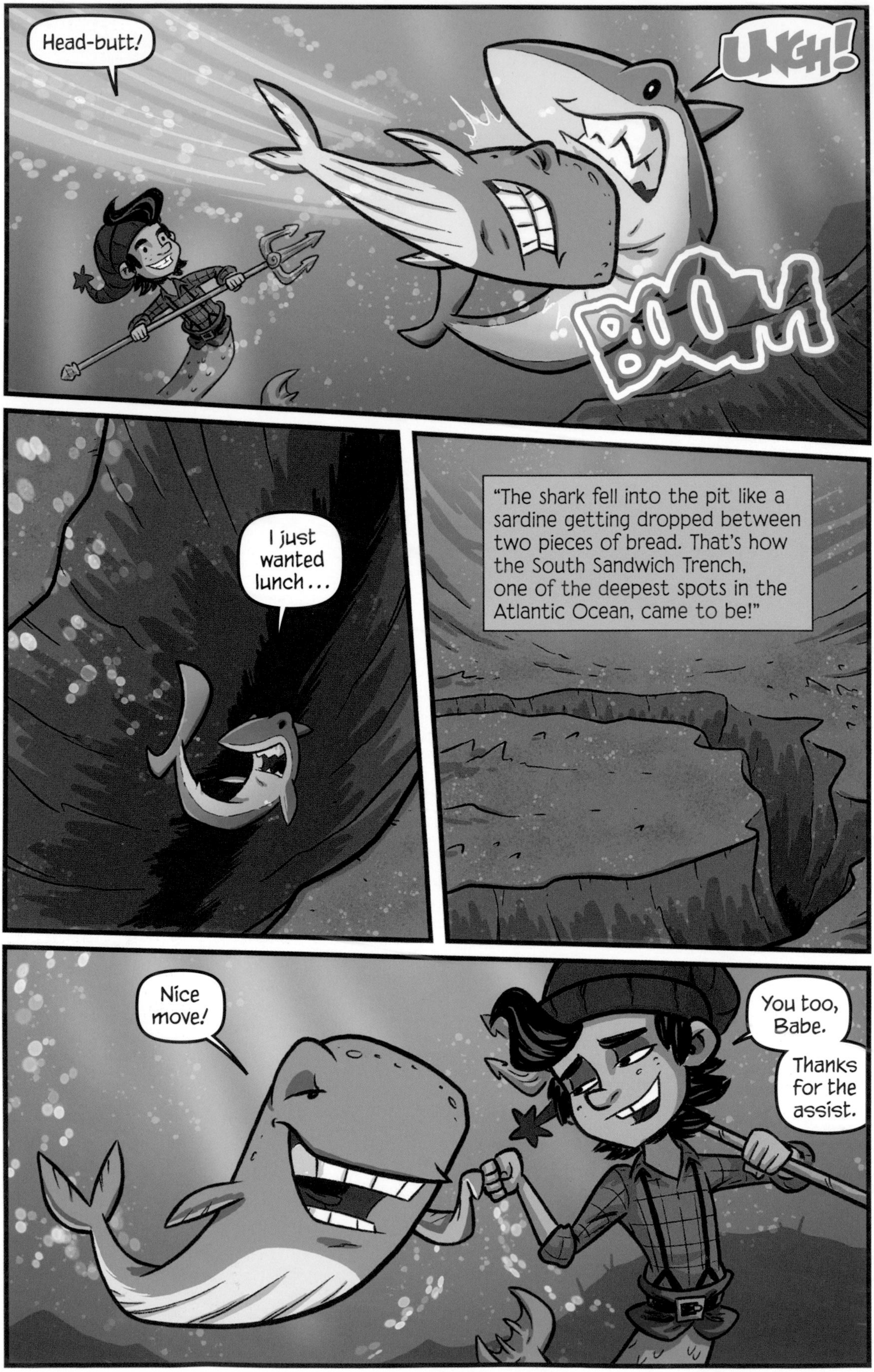

Head-butt!
UNGH!
BOOM
I just wanted lunch...
"The shark fell into the pit like a sardine getting dropped between two pieces of bread. That's how the South Sandwich Trench, one of the deepest spots in the Atlantic Ocean, came to be!"
Nice move!
You too, Babe.
Thanks for the assist.

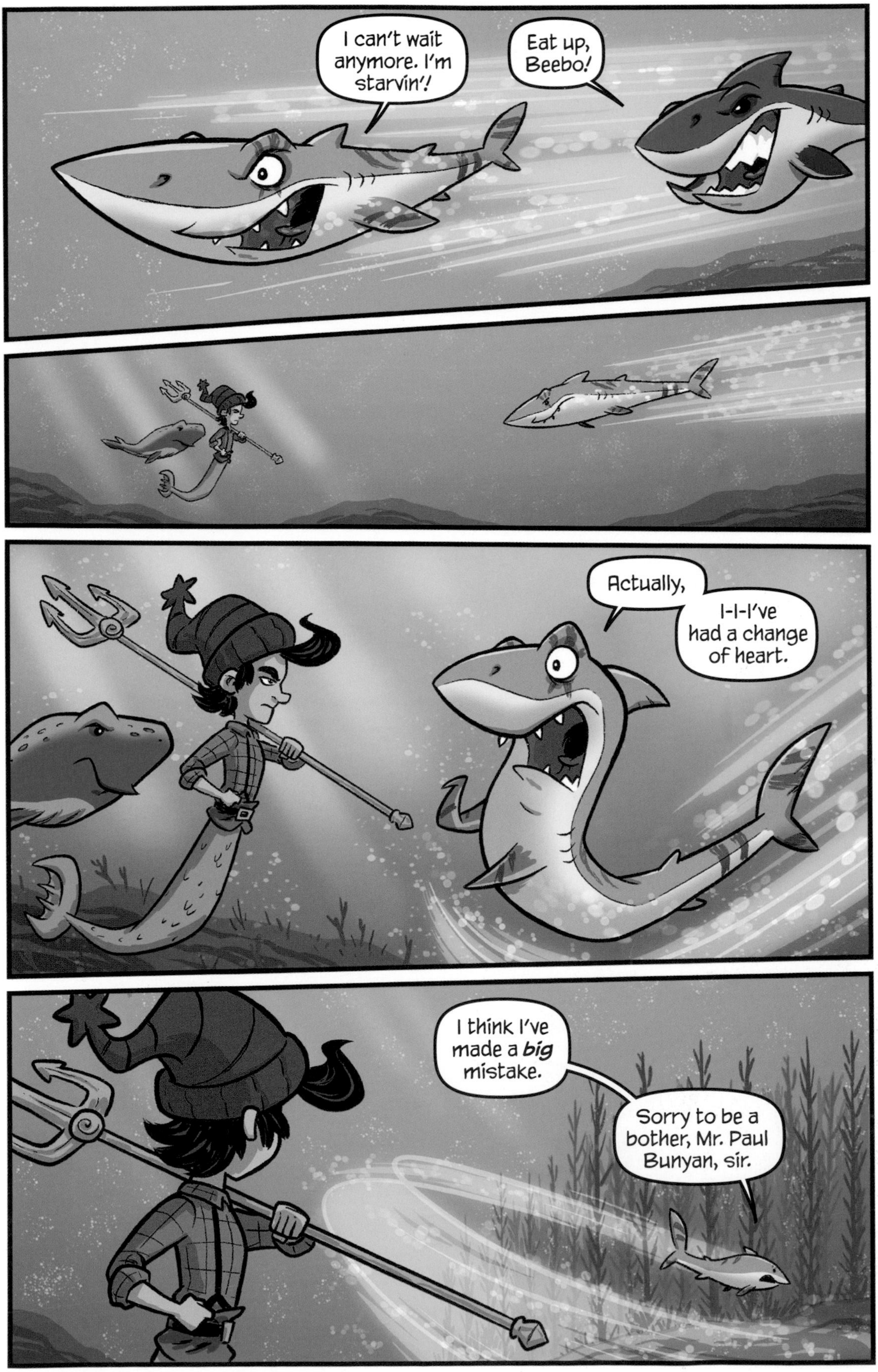
I can't wait anymore. I'm starvin'!
Eat up, Beebo!
Actually,
I-I-I've had a change of heart.
I think I've made a ***big*** mistake.
Sorry to be a bother, Mr. Paul Bunyan, sir.

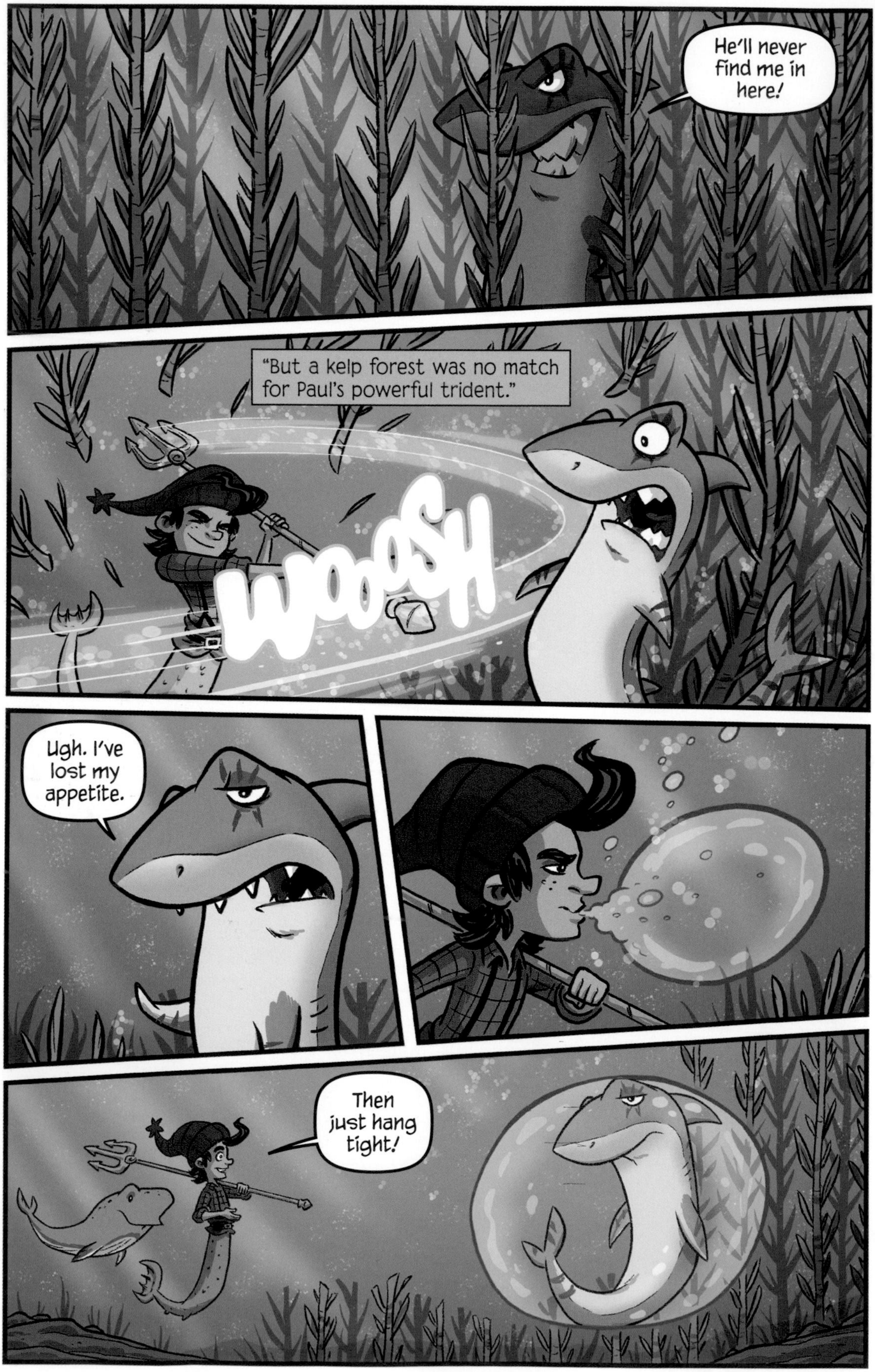

He'll never find me in here!
"But a kelp forest was no match for Paul's powerful trident."
WOOOSH
Ugh. I've lost my appetite.
Then just hang tight!

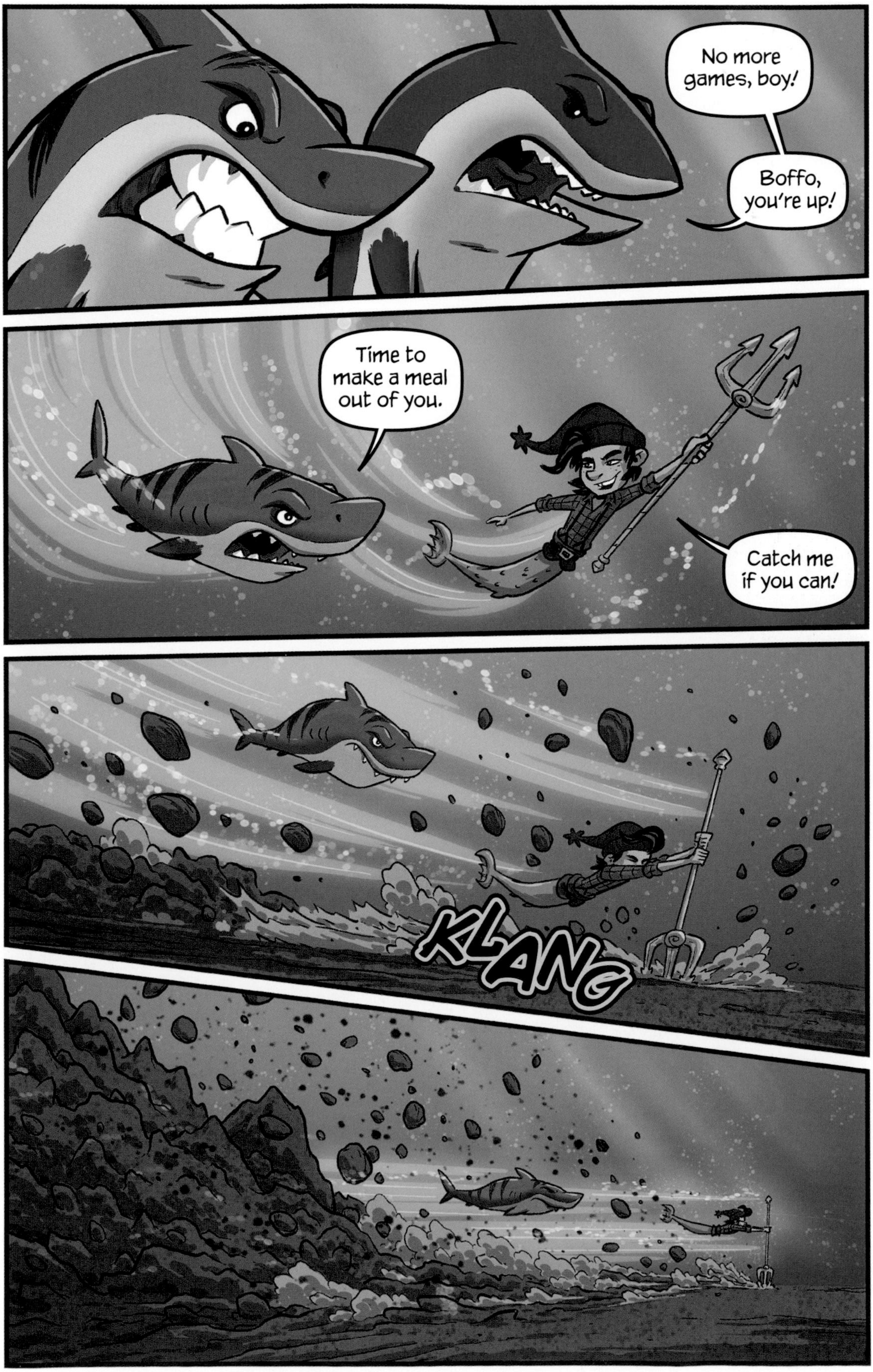
No more games, boy!
Boffo, you're up!
Time to make a meal out of you.
Catch me if you can!
KLANG

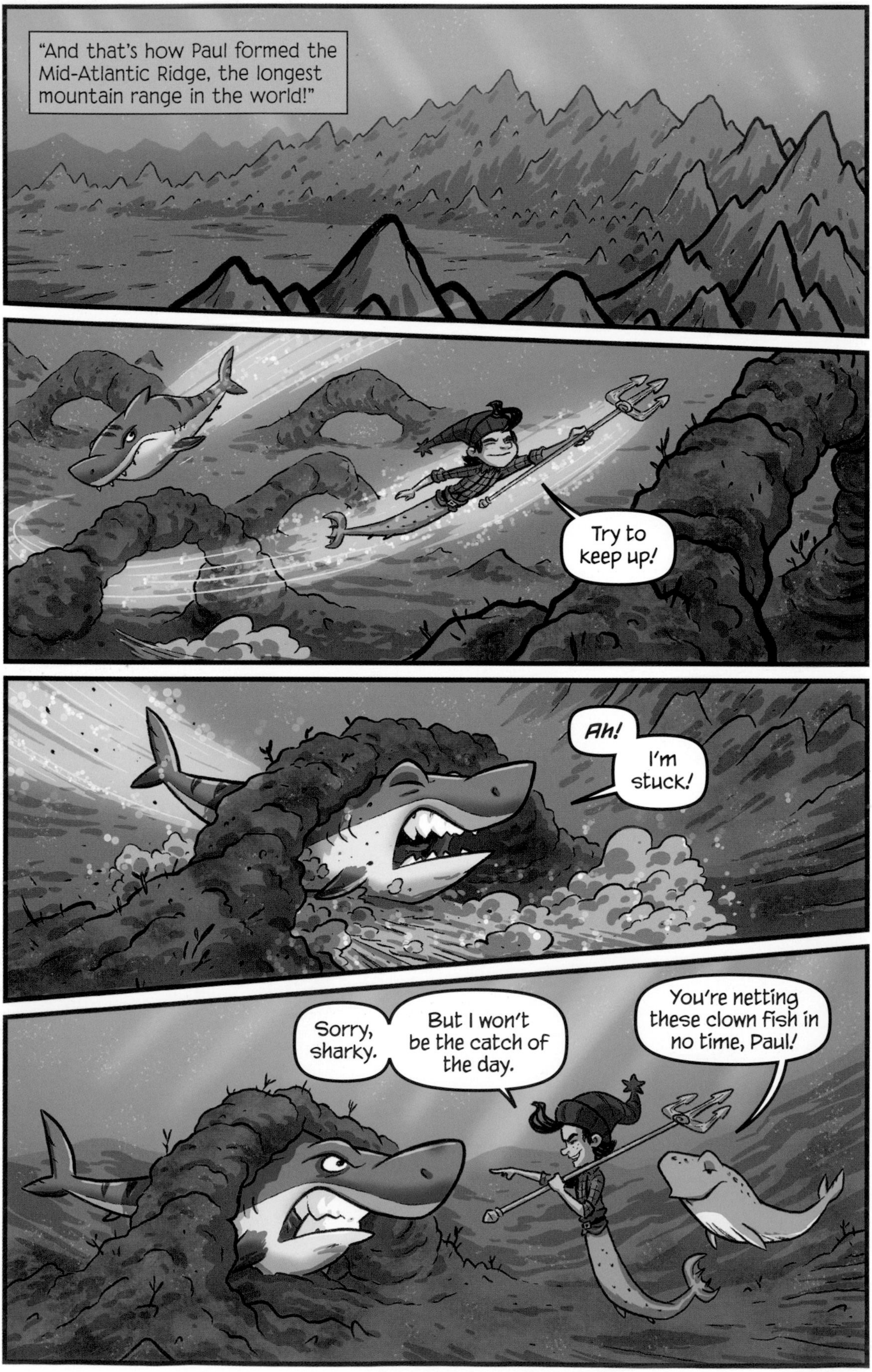
"And that's how Paul formed the Mid-Atlantic Ridge, the longest mountain range in the world!"
Try to keep up!
Ah!
I'm stuck!
Sorry, sharky.
But I won't be the catch of the day.
You're netting these clown fish in no time, Paul!

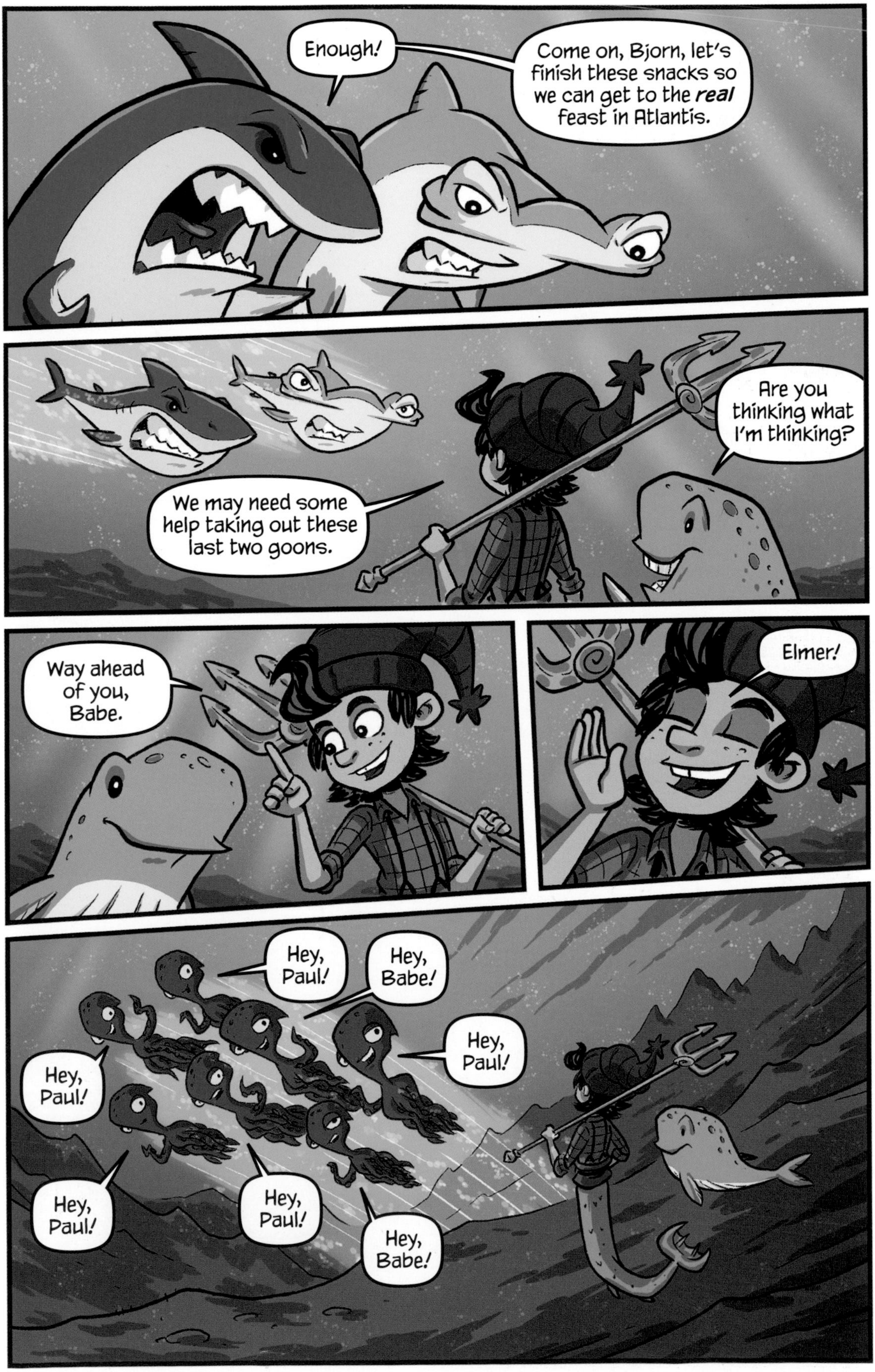
Enough!
Come on, Bjorn, let's finish these snacks so we can get to the *real* feast in Atlantis.
Are you thinking what I'm thinking?
We may need some help taking out these last two goons.
Way ahead of you, Babe.
Elmer!
Hey, Paul!
Hey, Babe!
Hey, Paul!
Hey, Paul!
Hey, Paul!
Hey, Paul!
Hey, Babe!

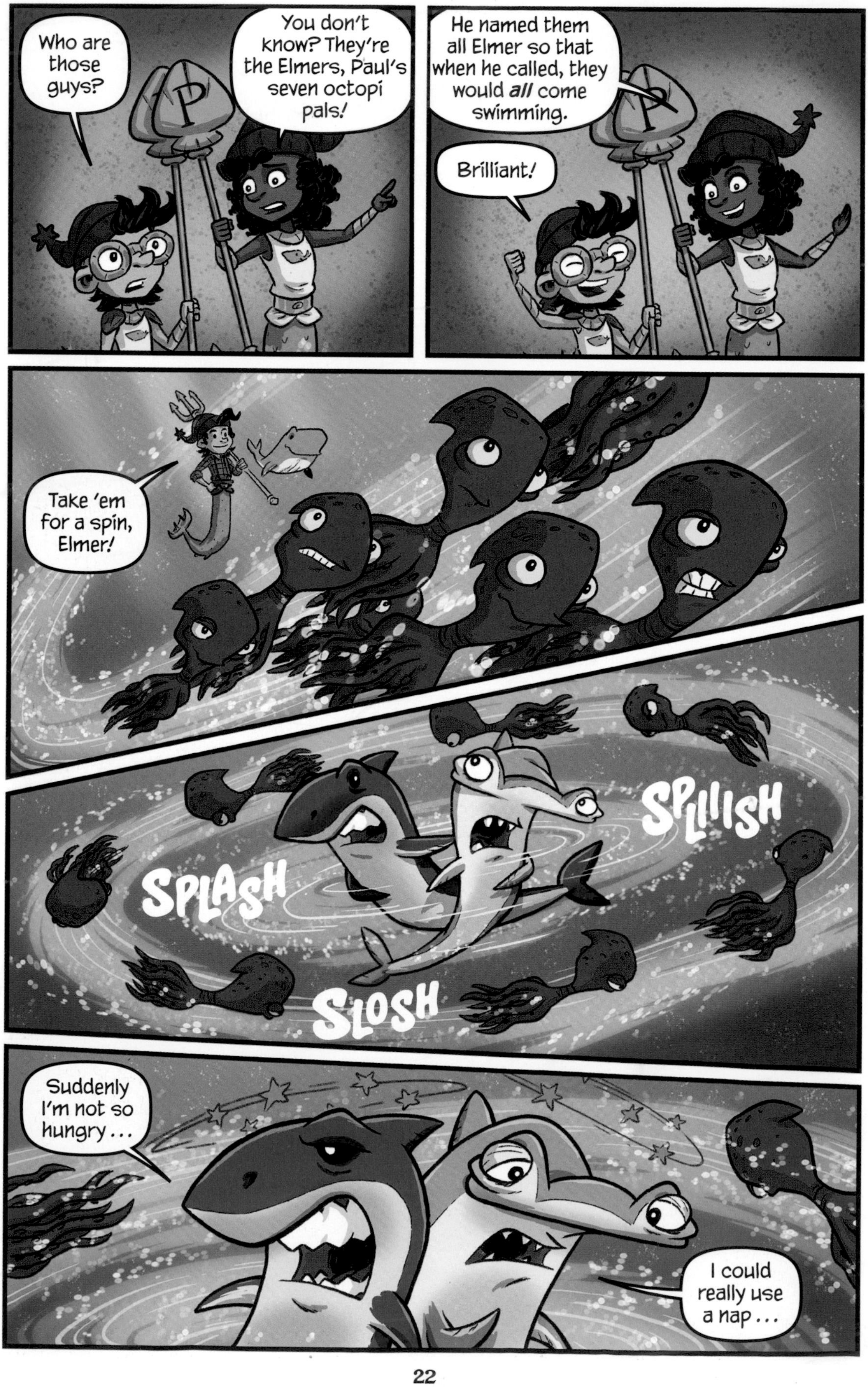

Who are those guys?
You don't know? They're the Elmers, Paul's seven octopi pals!
He named them all Elmer so that when he called, they would *all* come swimming.
Brilliant!
Take 'em for a spin, Elmer!
SPLASH
SPLIIISH
SLOSH
Suddenly I'm not so hungry . . .
I could really use a nap . . .

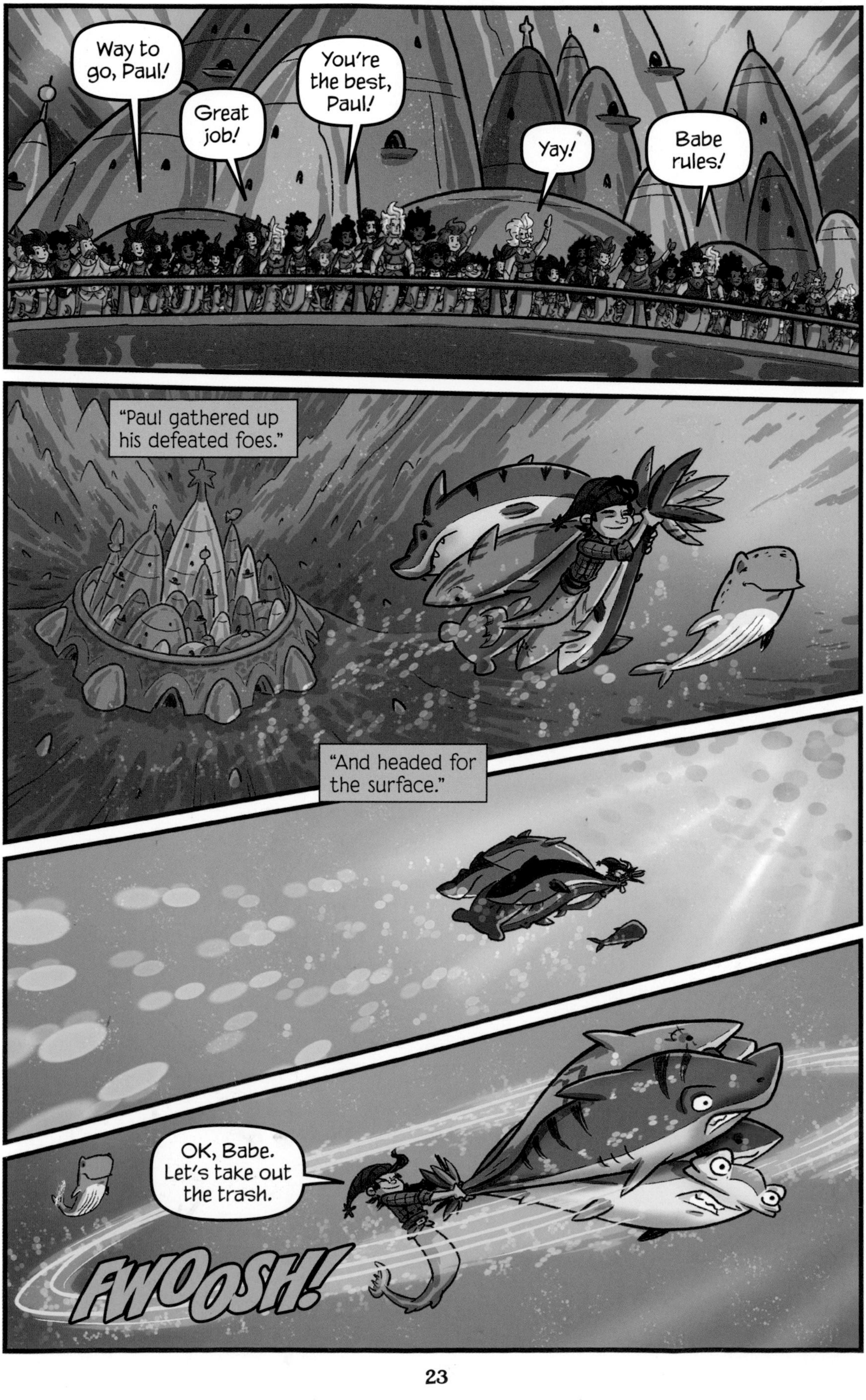
Way to go, Paul!
Great job!
You're the best, Paul!
Yay!
Babe rules!
"Paul gathered up his defeated foes."
"And headed for the surface."
OK, Babe. Let's take out the trash.
FWOOSH!

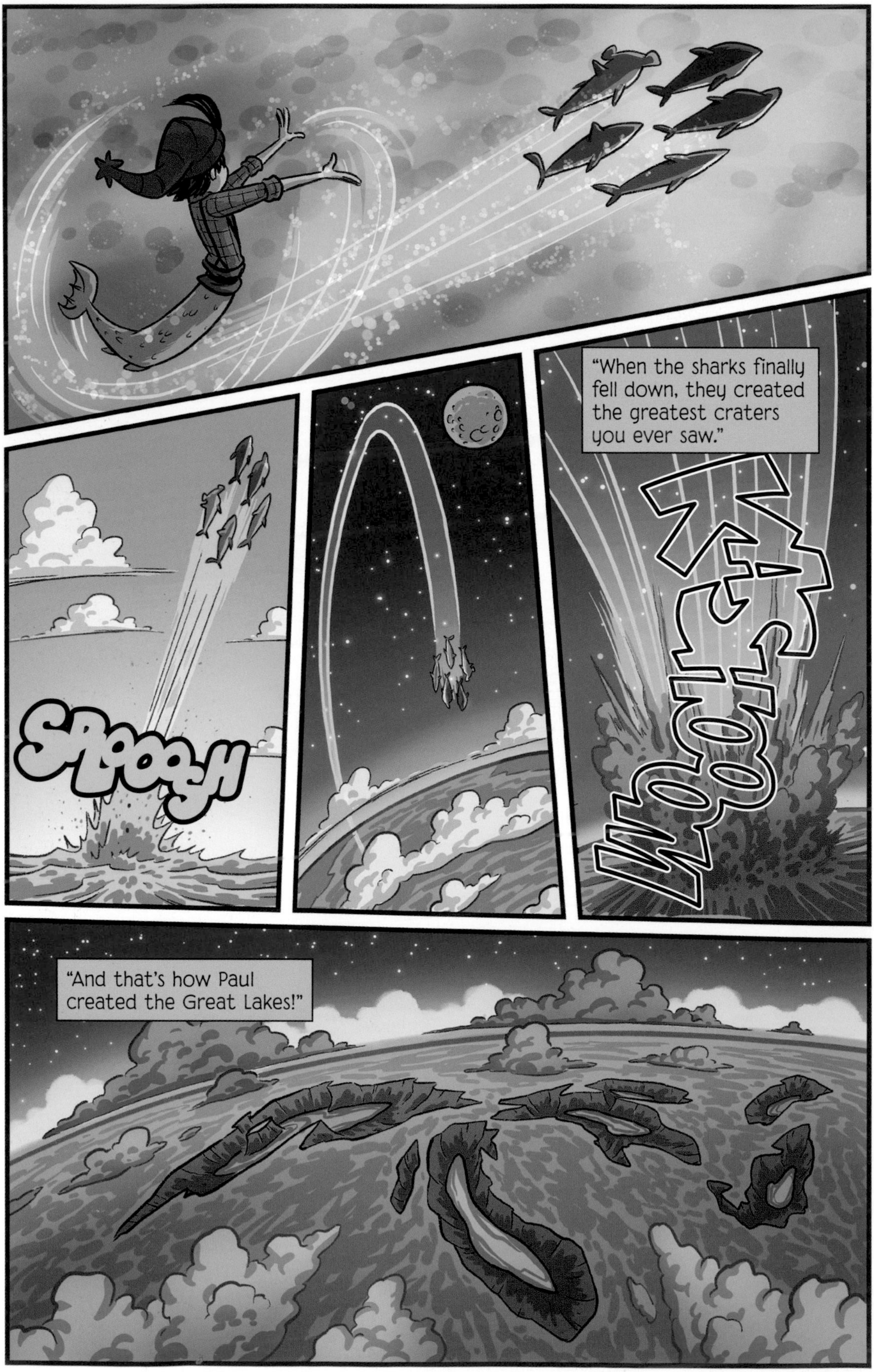
SPLOOOSH
"When the sharks finally fell down, they created the greatest craters you ever saw."
KA-CHOOOM
"And that's how Paul created the Great Lakes!"

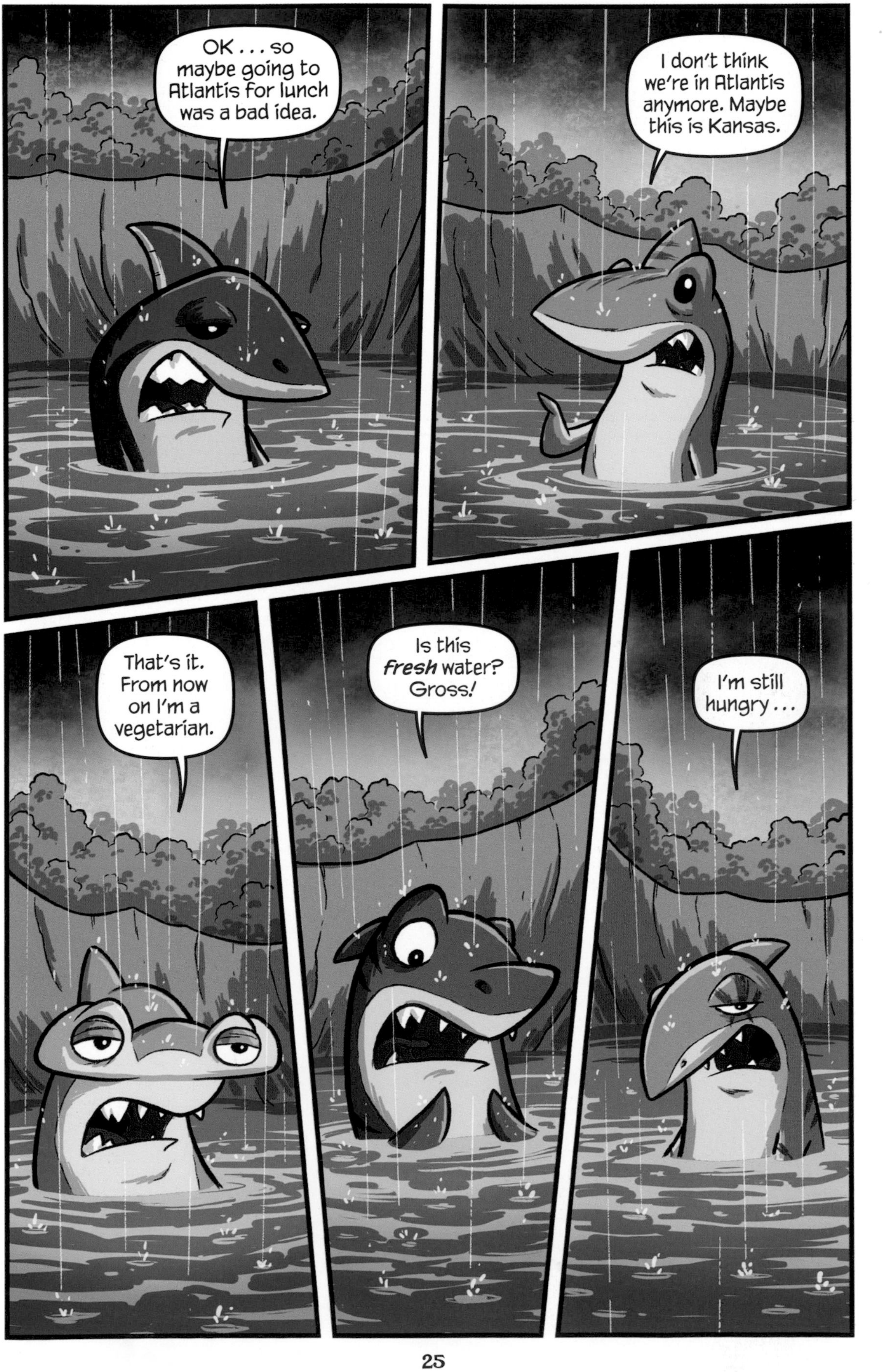

OK . . . so maybe going to Atlantis for lunch was a bad idea.
I don't think we're in Atlantis anymore. Maybe this is Kansas.
That's it. From now on I'm a vegetarian.
Is this *fresh* water? Gross!
I'm still hungry . . .

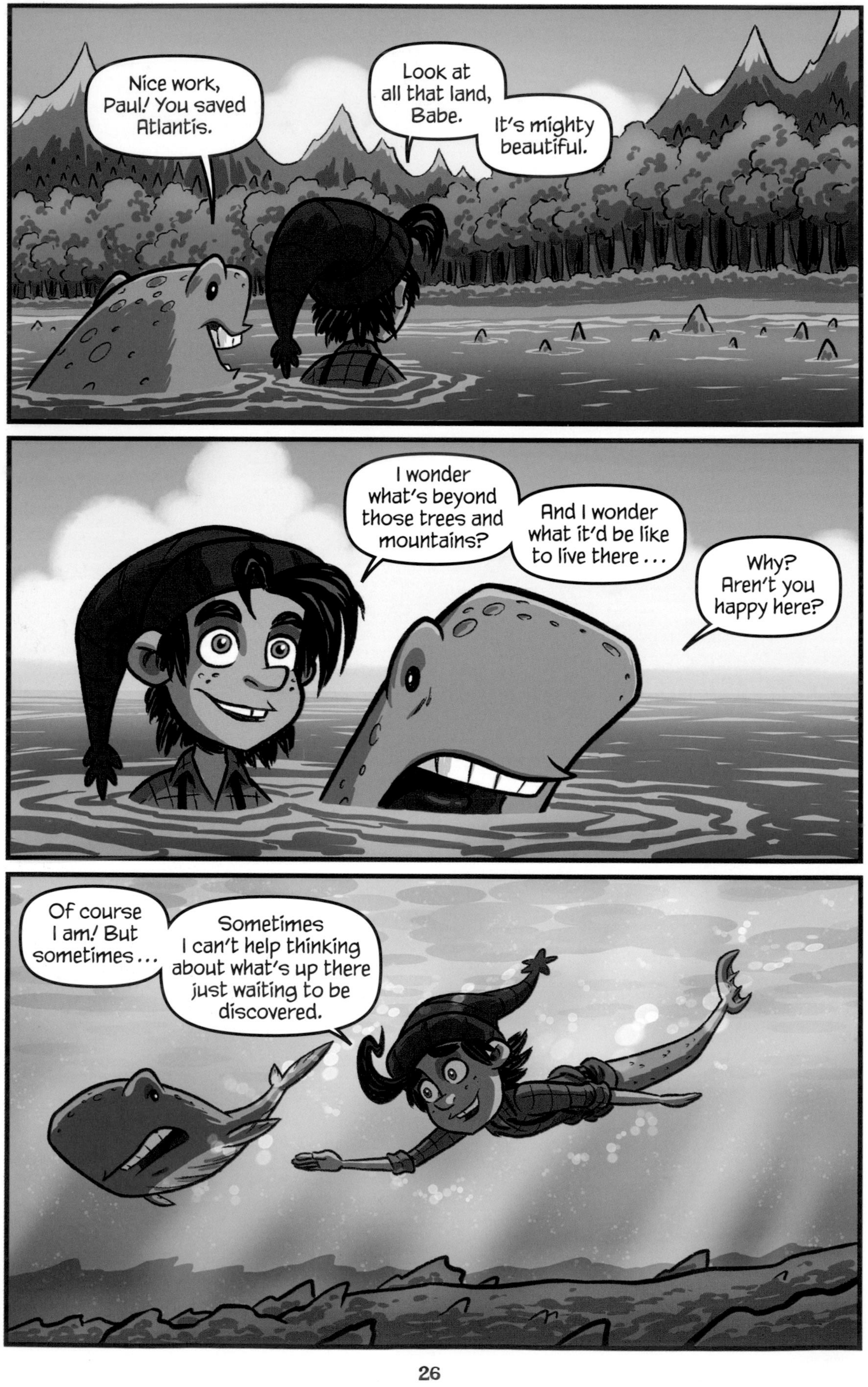
Nice work, Paul! You saved Atlantis.
Look at all that land, Babe.
It's mighty beautiful.
I wonder what's beyond those trees and mountains?
And I wonder what it'd be like to live there . . .
Why? Aren't you happy here?
Of course I am! But sometimes . . .
Sometimes I can't help thinking about what's up there just waiting to be discovered.

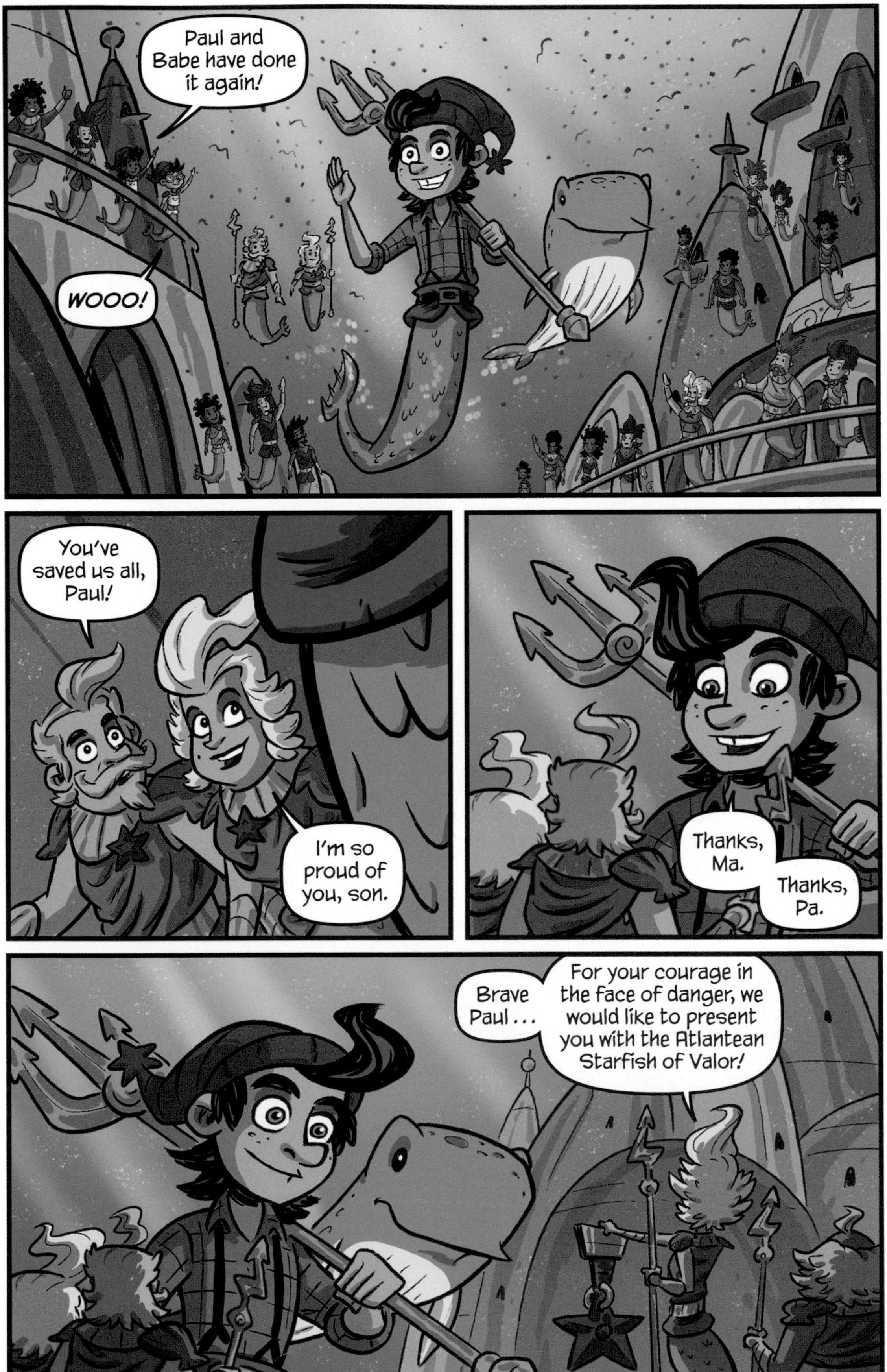

Paul and Babe have done it again!
WOOO!
You've saved us all, Paul!
I'm so proud of you, son.
Thanks, Ma.
Thanks, Pa.
Brave Paul . . .
For your courage in the face of danger, we would like to present you with the Atlantean Starfish of Valor!

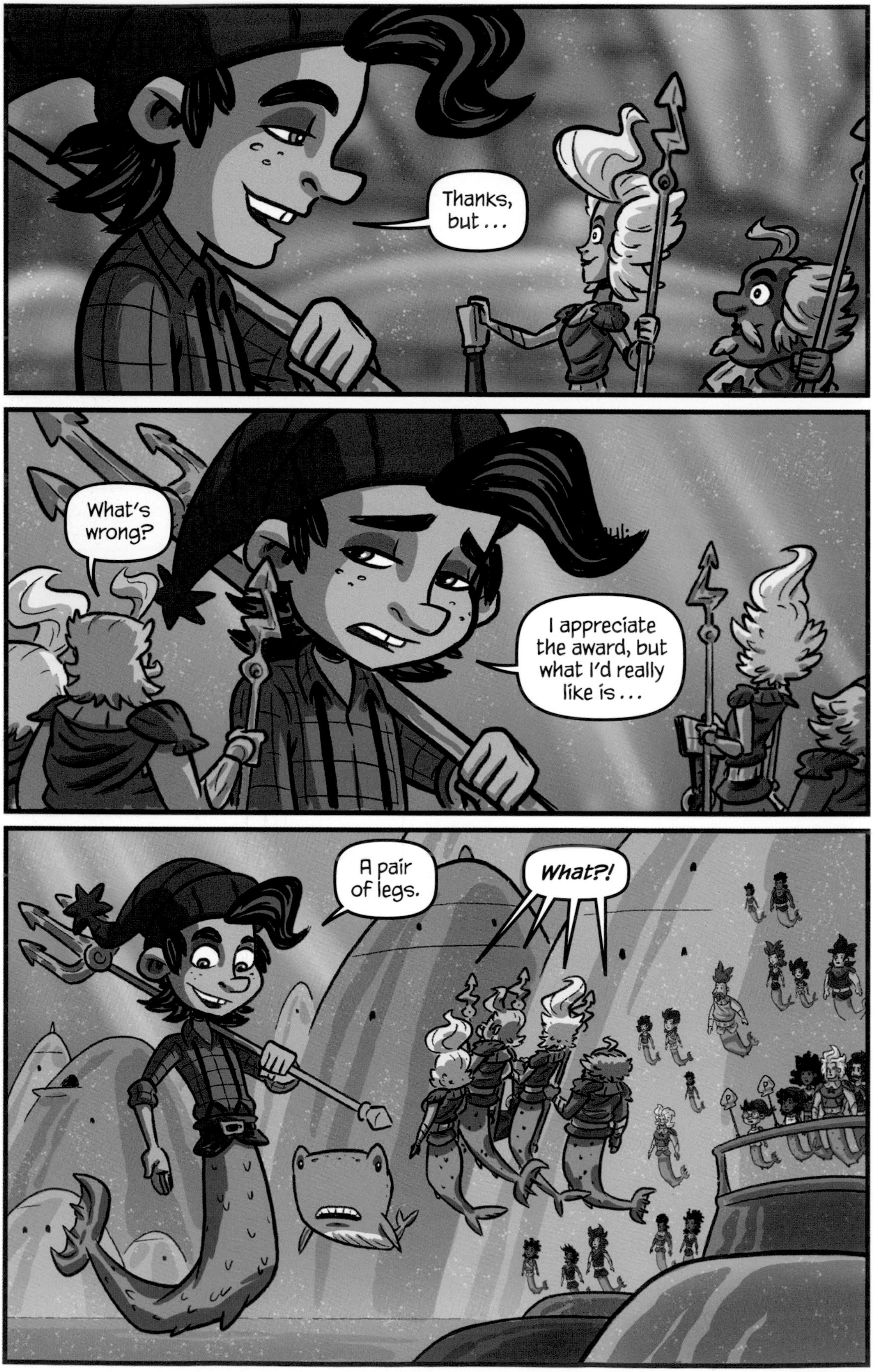
Thanks, but . . .
What's wrong?
I appreciate the award, but what I'd really like is . . .
A pair of legs.
What?!

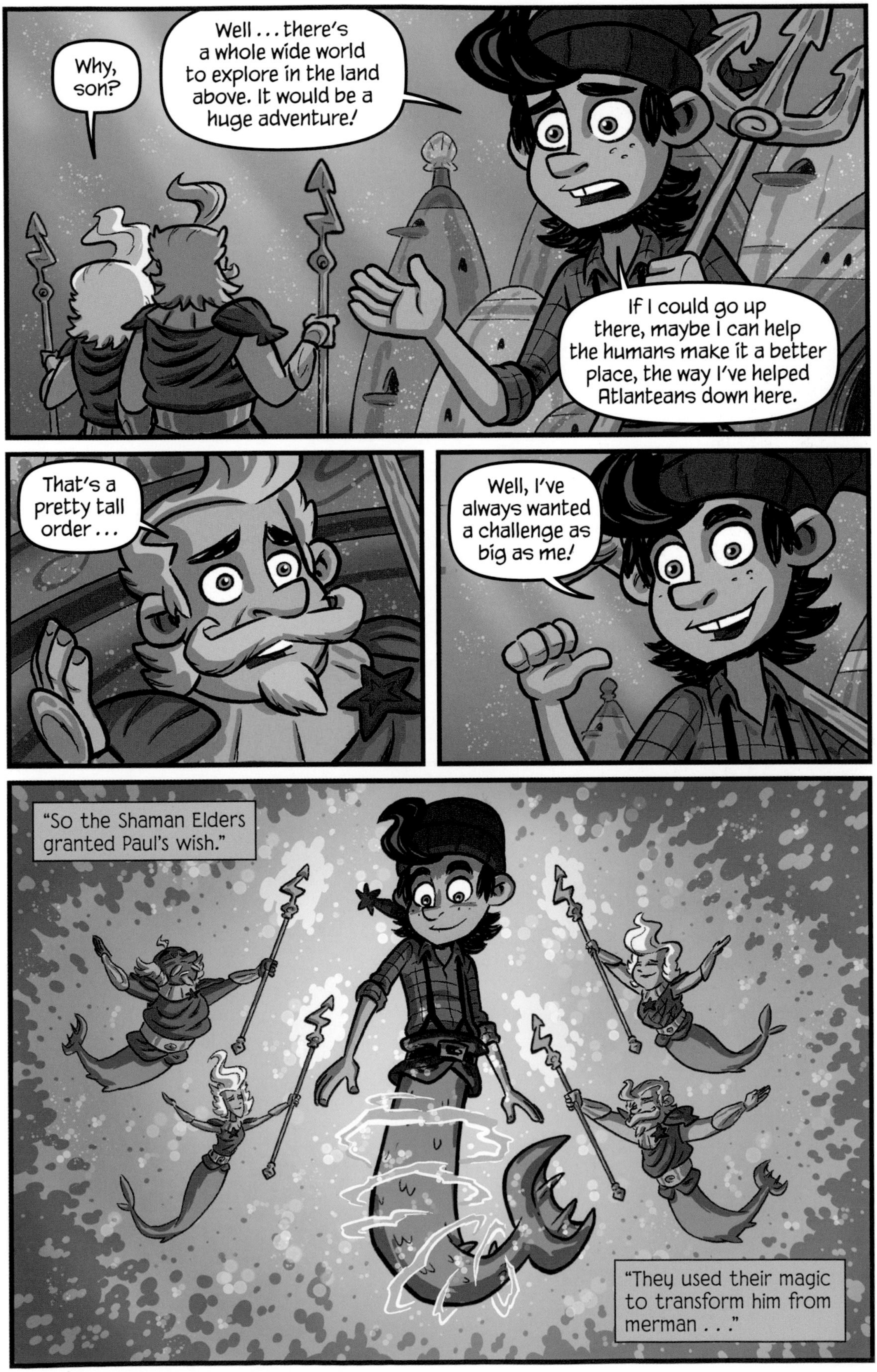
Why, son?
Well . . . there's a whole wide world to explore in the land above. It would be a huge adventure!
If I could go up there, maybe I can help the humans make it a better place, the way I've helped Atlanteans down here.
That's a pretty tall order . . .
Well, I've always wanted a challenge as big as me!
"So the Shaman Elders granted Paul's wish."
"They used their magic to transform him from merman . . ."

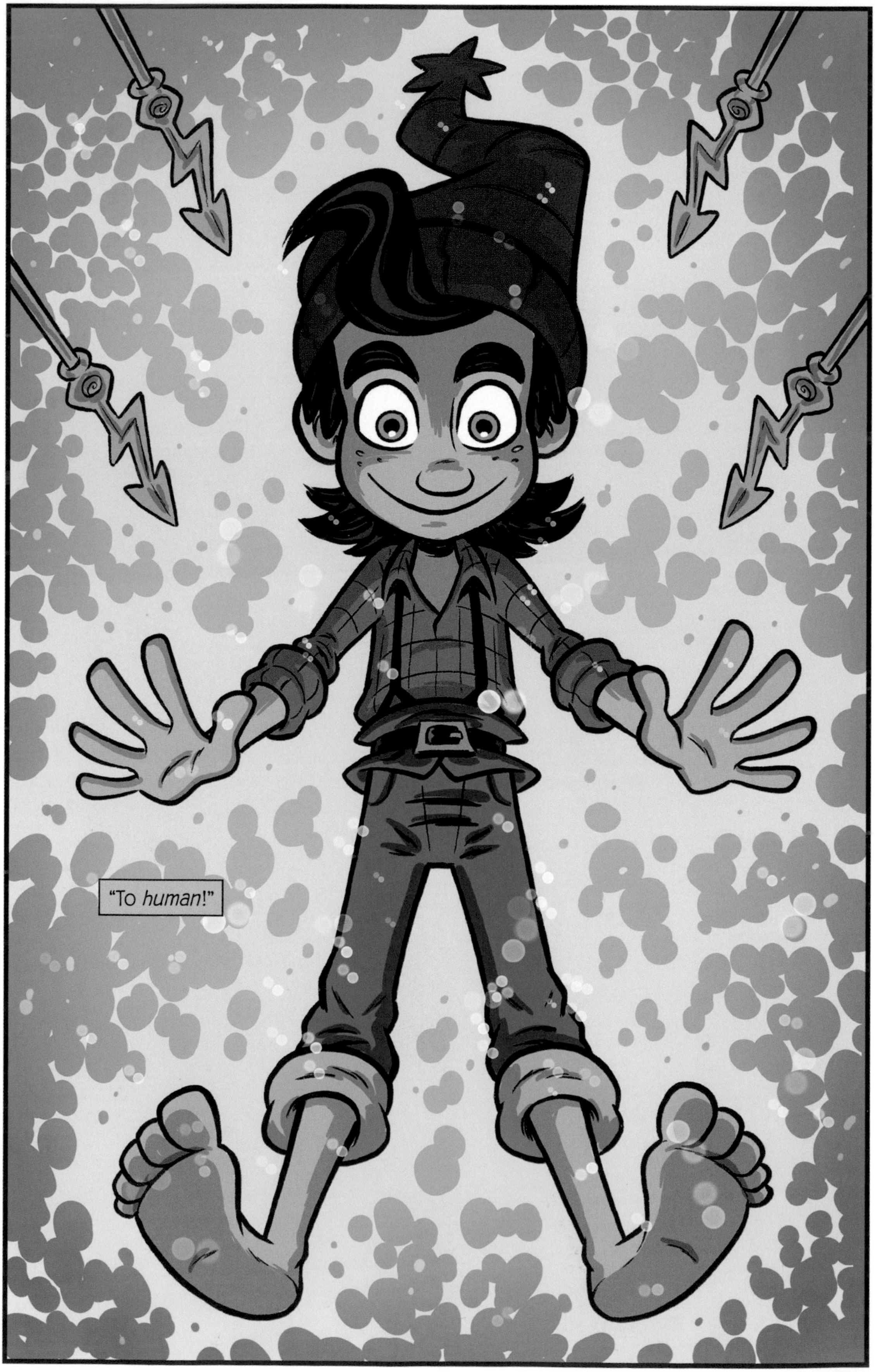
"To *human*!"

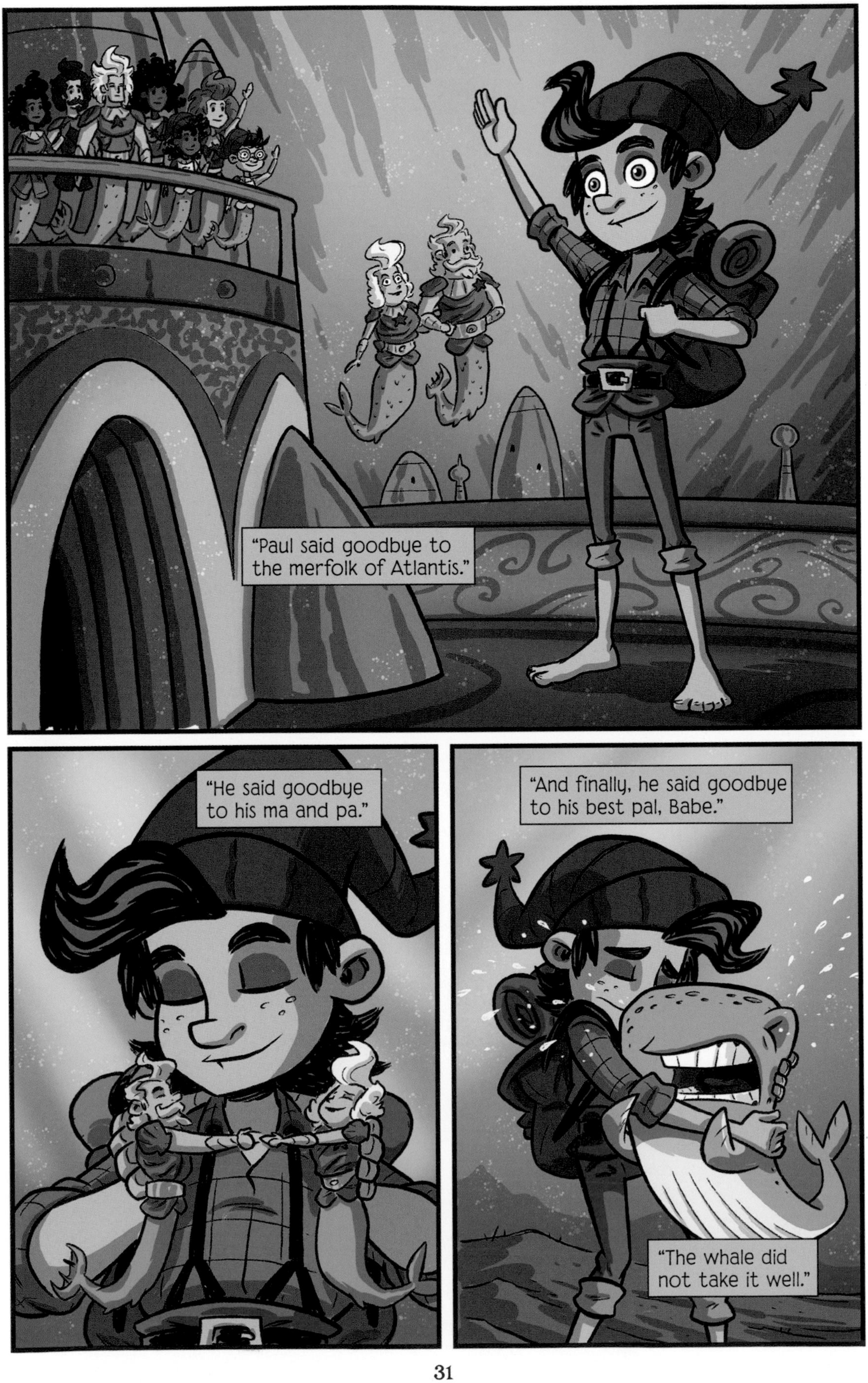
"Paul said goodbye to the merfolk of Atlantis."
"He said goodbye to his ma and pa."
"And finally, he said goodbye to his best pal, Babe."
"The whale did not take it well."

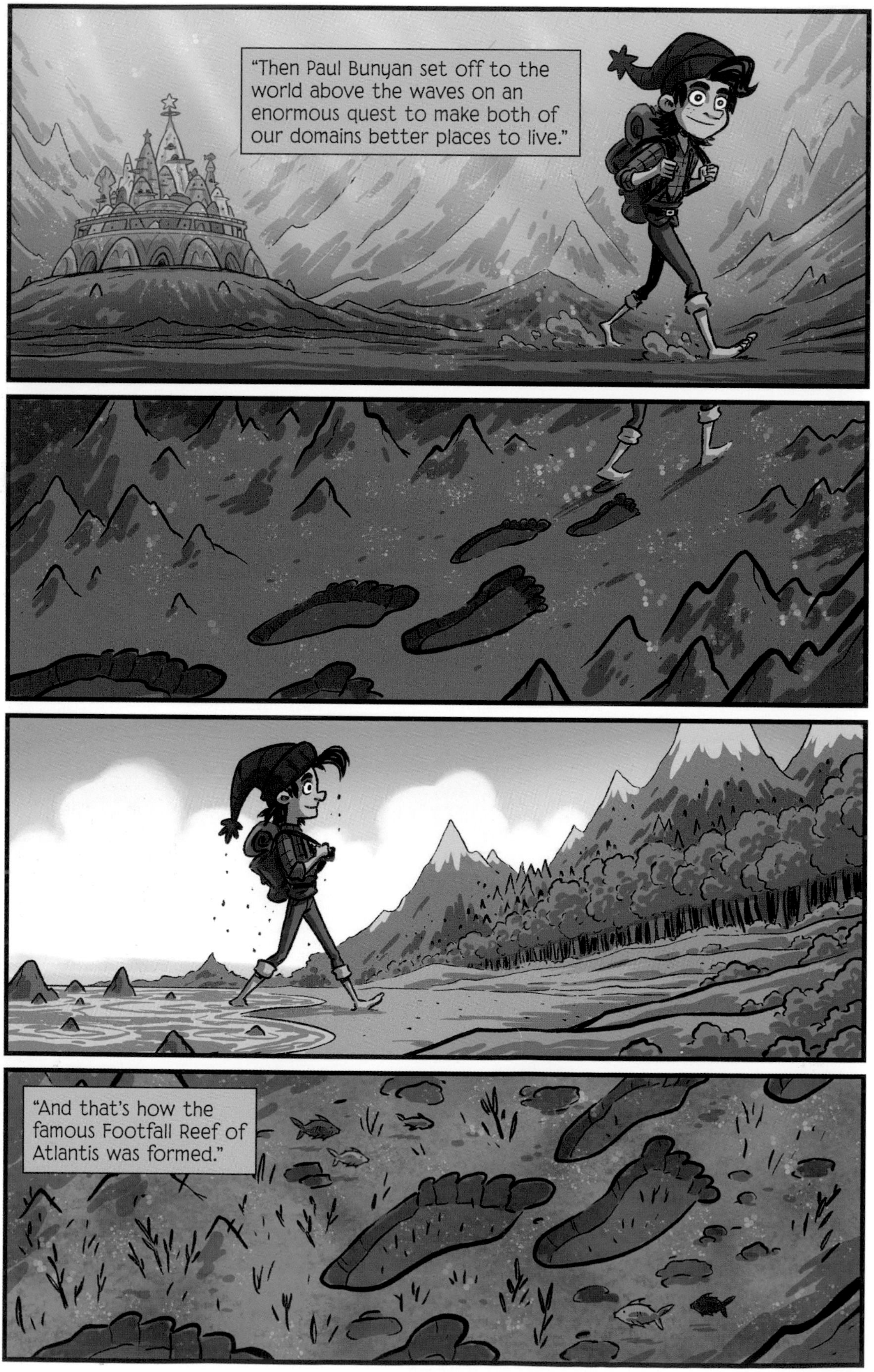
"Then Paul Bunyan set off to the world above the waves on an enormous quest to make both of our domains better places to live."
"And that's how the famous Footfall Reef of Atlantis was formed."

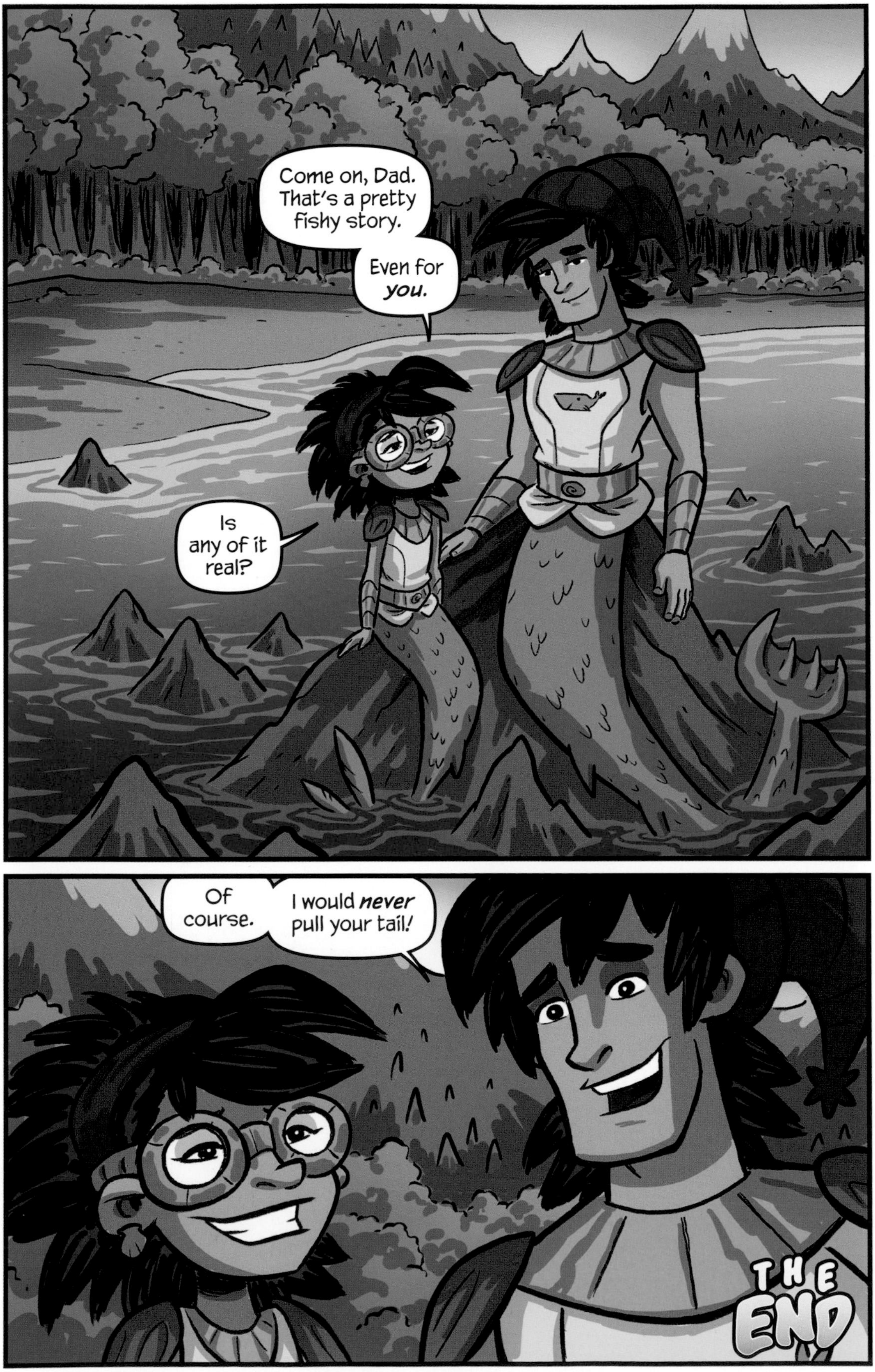
Come on, Dad. That's a pretty fishy story.
Even for *you.*
Is any of it real?
Of course.
I would *never* pull your tail!
THE END

ALL ABOUT THE ORIGINAL TALE!

A folktale is a story that's told over and over again and passed down through generations. Some say the tale of the giant lumberjack Paul Bunyan was created by loggers around the Great Lakes area. But the legend became widely known after a lumber company started using the big man in their ads in 1914. In the original tale, Paul Bunyan doesn't face mega-sharks, but he does have larger-than-life adventures.

When Paul Bunyan was born, he was already so big that five storks had to carry him to his parents. Then the boy grew up—way, way up! He used wagon wheels instead of buttons on his shirts.

Paul's extreme height and strength made him a natural lumberjack. He could chop down an acre of trees with a single swing of his ax. Paul logged the forests of the northern United States and had a crew to help him. There were the Seven Axemen, each named Elmer. When Paul hollered, "Elmer!" they all came running. The cook Sourdough Sam made monstrous pancakes with a griddle so big, men greased it by strapping bacon onto their feet and skating on the metal.

One winter when the snowflakes were blue, Paul found a trapped baby ox. He rescued the fella, but the ox was stained blue by the snow. Paul named him Babe. Except Babe grew to be almost as big as Paul! The two became best friends and a great logging team.

Paul and Babe had many adventures. They fought off swarms of mosquito-bee critters. They cleared all the trees from North and South Dakota to ready the land for farming. Their mighty footprints created the 10,000 lakes of Minnesota, and just by dragging his ax on the ground, Paul created the Grand Canyon.

A **FAR OUT** GUIDE TO THE TALE'S UNDERWATER TWISTS!

In this tale, Paul Bunyan isn't a huge man with an ax. He's a giant merboy with a trident!

Sea creatures replace the original Paul's crew. The blue ox becomes a blue whale, and the Seven Axemen become the Seven Octopi.

Instead of shaping the land above water, Paul creates ocean floor features like the Mid-Atlantic Ridge and the South Sandwich Trench.

Paul chops down trees in the traditional story. Here he uses his size to protect the people of Atlantis.

VISUAL QUESTIONS

1

Why do you think the color is different in this panel? How does it connect to what's happening in the story? (Check page 12 to refresh your memory.) Try to find other spots where this effect is used.

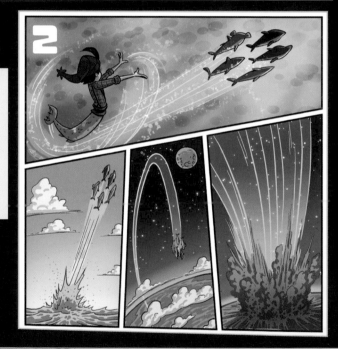

2

Comics can express a lot of information in just a few images. Look at this sequence (or turn to page 24), and write a couple of paragraphs that describe the action. Be sure to make it exciting!

3

Folktales sometimes explain how natural formations came to be. In this version, Paul Bunyan creates many underwater features. Do some research and find a unique feature in the ocean. Write your own tale about how merman Paul creates it.

Why does Beebo decide not to attack Paul and Babe? Use examples from the text and art to support your answer.

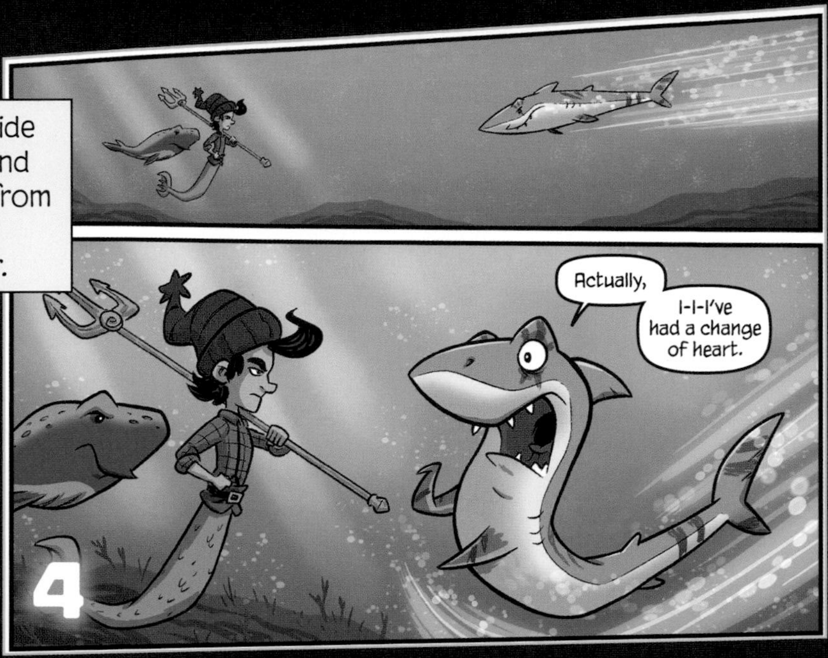
Actually,
I-I-I've had a change of heart.
4

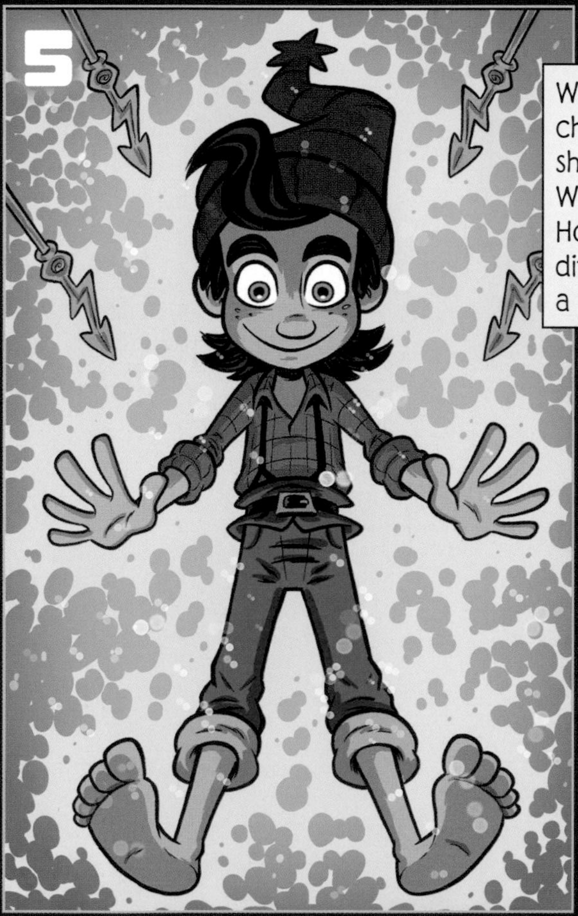
5

Why do you think the creators chose to use a full page to show Paul's transformation? What feeling does it create? How would the scene be different if it were shown in a small panel? Talk about it!

In the original and this far out version, Paul Bunyan and Babe are great pals. Flip through the story and find at least two examples where you can see their friendship.

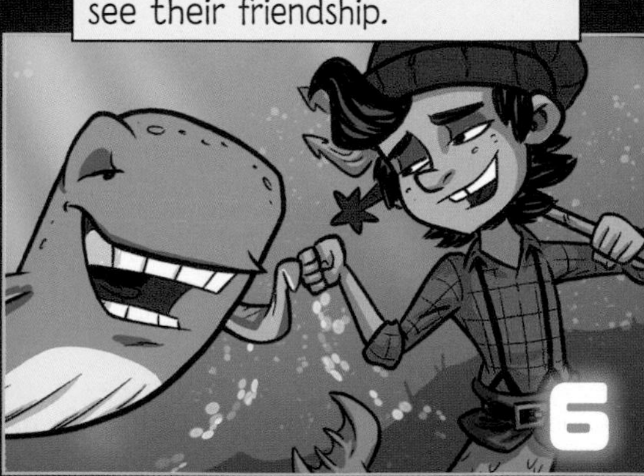
6

AUTHOR

Penelope Gruber writes stories for young readers. She's worked on a variety of books but likes creating comics most of all. She lives in Minnesota, where it's said that Paul Bunyan's giant footsteps created the state's famous ten thousand lakes.

ILLUSTRATOR

Otis Frampton is a comic book writer and illustrator. He is also one of the character and background artists on the popular animated web series How It Should Have Ended. His comic book series Oddly Normal was published by Image Comics.

GLOSSARY

assist (uh-SIST)—to help another person with something

brigade (bri-GAYD)—a group of people that have come together for a special purpose

crater (KRAY-tur)—a large hole in the ground caused by big rocks (or sharks!) crashing into Earth's surface

defeat (di-FEET)—to win over someone else; to beat

domain (doh-MAYN)—an area under the control of a ruler or particular group

explore (ik-SPLOR)—to travel through a place in order to learn more about it

inseparable (in-SEP-er-uh-buhl)—impossible to keep apart

quest (KWEST)—a journey to do or find something

shaman (SHAH-muhn)—a leader of a group who uses magic in different ways, such as healing people and seeing into the future

transform (trans-FORM)—to change completely

trench (TRENCH)—a long, deep, narrow hole in the ocean floor

trident (TRY-dent)—a long spear with three sharp points at its end

vegetarian (vej-uh-TAIR-ee-uhn)—a person who does not eat meat

TRULY LEGENDARY TALES

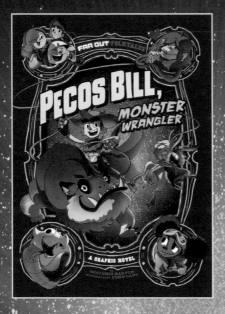

FAR OUT FOLKTALES